CAPREOL

Also by Richard Williamson

THE DAWN IS MY BROTHER

Capreol

The Story of a Roebuck

Richard Williamson

Illustrations by David Carl Forbes

MACDONALD · LONDON

Dedicated to the memory of a great man

First published 1973
by Macdonald and Jane's
St Giles House
49/50 Poland Street, London, W.1

ISBN 0 356 04574 9

Set and printed in Great Britain by
Tonbridge Printers Ltd, Peach Hall Works, Tonbridge, Kent

Contents

There is a road that turning always
Cuts off the country of Again.
Archers stand there on every side
And as it runs Time's deer is slain,
And lies where it has lain.

Edwin Muir (*1887–1959*)
'The Road', from 'The Collected Poems, 1921–58'

YEAR ONE
GYRLE

Chapter One

Night coming in the valley, a rind of moon behind the beech hanger on the hill and a woodcock rising from a holly thicket into the hoar air.

Each evening since the early year the woodcock had flighted from the roost of holly leaves and flown beyond the hill to the copse called Blackbush where the mould was soft beneath the oaks and sycamores.

Now the crows came slipping in to their winter roost in the yew forest of the valley slopes, passing below, and the woodcock turned and flew, not to Blackbush, but around the valley, out of sight to the ground. In the high air where sometimes frost formed across the flight feathers of its wing, the woodcock was in sight of the spring moon beyond the hanger. It uttered a soft whistle, then a grunt; soft whistle, then a grunt; a squeaking like a bat, a croaking like a frog; the only song it had. Now and then it was heard far below. It had found a warm air.

In the night, late, when the winter stars of Orion had gone, a movement in the valley, unheard. The crows felt it in the yew bowers, and talked of it, and shook their heads back beneath their wings, and woke again for talk, all through the dark hours. A boar badger, worm hunting in the oak mould, stopped many times to listen. Other birds there were, thrushes in the bramble thickets, a wren that sang suddenly from a crevice in the oldest yew, and a white owl that hunted the rough grassy hollows between the forest of yew trees.

On that night the woodcock did not travel on along the hill ridge to Blackbush but after circling the lower valley landed beneath a small thicket that lay apart from the yew forest, out in the grassy glade. Here it crept among oak leaves to search for worms. Forty years the oak had grown there, sheltered from sheep and rabbits when a seedling by the boughs of a yew. When the sheep had gone, and rabbits lay dead of plague, fourteen years before, other trees had grown round the two. There was spindle and the ruby stems of dogwood, privet, ash and buckthorn, and a dogrose that hung scarlet hips across them all at Michaelmas.

At woodcock light, a roe deer, a doe, rose from a bed of yew needles in the forest of Windens. The moon in Windens, at its spring rising, had begun to lose the white brilliance of winter. Its yellowing light glowed through the downy leaves of birch and chestnut, and made stippled shapes on the boles of trees and on the old leaf pattern of the forest floor. Once Windens had been quiet, with cover in the beech and spruce trees, and the greater depths of the yew groves enclosed within the plantation. Then the wood was felled, and replanted, but the new trees gave little cover as yet, and the deer were frightened of the daylight.

The doe had been uncertain for her young, so she had left the place where she had been born two years before and walked out of the valleys of the down slope, following the wind. From the old coppice woods of East Holte where blue bell leaves were throwing off a slough of dead oak mould she crossed the down at Manna Ash, and followed the running darkness of the hedgerow or the streams of air that sluiced between tree boles, as a salmon follows the currents of a river. She was a little thing of the night, no more a brown swift animal; gentle, staring at everything that might have moved. After the high down she came into a wood at Stonerock, where ash and oak tree grew, and there was the scent of a buck that was rattling young trees about with his antlers.

The ash twigs pierced the sky like tridents, but their outlines were blurred with flower buds; as the three-prong tines of the roebuck were hung with velvet. Beneath the purple flower-clustered ash the roebuck was searching for an ash sapling. The roebuck's antlers itched with the hot blood that formed their growth: they must be rubbed clean. He found the tree, an ash sapling of twelve summers and with no flowers, scarred down one side and half covered with a new callous of bark, and stepping with high steps over the bramble strands which had formed in the twelve months since he had last sought the tree, he rubbed his antlers, fraying off the new bark, bending the sapling.

The doe walked on silently, knowing the buck, the father of the young within her womb, but not wanting any contact. He watched her go, marking her way, knowing that he would find her again after the time of birth.

The deer path led between bramble and young trees, and had changed but slightly over the years, following the lines of ash. The path was marked with the longer slots of fallow deer which had passed three nights before.

The doe moved through the wood, with muzzle constantly touching grasses of the deer path for scent. Once a dog barked and rattled a chain by some cottages, but she ignored the sound. Thereafter she stopped many times in the silence of the night to taste the air with small black muzzle uplifted. She moved slowly, searching with care among the patterns of light and shade made by the moon, before taking a bramble leaf or a black ash bud.

A fox made her start – she knew the rich rank smell but had not heard the fox approach. Now ears were strained to hear the scratching of a single bramble thorn on hair and the twitching of old ash keys under pads as the vixen slid by, dark on the forest floor, skirting the pools of light. She had come nearly half a mile from her cubs at Blackbush on the way to a meadow where mice could be pounced upon. She had watched, then half circled the doe, instinctively curious of the quiet movements among the trees which she had not been completely certain were those of a deer. The doe blew the heavy smell from her nostrils and plucked a dogwood leaf. Bank voles scuttled the dead leaves. A moth burred past. The old scents of day and the new scents of night were taken with the pungent tastes of chewed leaves; nothing was missed. The doe stared at the new scents and sounds, but her eyes merely reflected on the information from nose and ears.

A wood pigeon flapped a wing in half-sleep high up in the ash trees over the deer path. The bird was one of many that had clattered among the ash branches at dusk, its crop bulging with clover and the purple ash flowers. It awoke and peered at the ground when a badger, digging for worms, scattered stones and earth over the bushes. The doe had winded the badger already, but kept still even after the pigeon had sunk its head in crop, with closed eyes.

The deer path was trajoined by lesser paths where roe

had wandered in curiosity or searched out a special leaf. There was a path that led to a sallow willow bush, stunted in growth by the continued nibblings of a fallow doe who loved the acrid-tasting bark. Occasionally in winter she had led others to the bush when there were no leaves, but the others had snorted as their muzzles touched the willow's bark.

The way led up the slope of the hill to Blackbush, to dense bramble thickets where only the deer and foxes and badgers went: where the antlers of fallow were all but hidden when they walked. When the doe came to a rideway at the top of the hill she hesitated before leaving the bramble thicket. She stared at the dim grass track, while the moon moved a branch shadow across her back. A hedgesparrow woke suddenly and sang its spring song that was like the sound of a stream rambling down its stony bed. Death-watch beetles ticked in an old ash post.

She moved into the ride, recoiling at the stronger scents, then bounded across, leaving slots in the soft earth of the ride that showed cleaves widely splayed and the marks of the dew claws. With the sixth bound the doe cleared a wire-netting fence into a plantation whose bark had been stripped, which was now dying brown at its tip. The plantation was eight years old: some of the trees were higher than a man. They had been planted where oaks and hazel had been felled. Oak stools showed here and there, and were used by the pheasants as sunning platforms. The hazel stumps had sent up shoots again. Clematis and wild woodbine entwined some of the trees: grasses grew tall with nettles and a few thin bluebells. There were bramble beds and dog-rose, all had sprung when the trees were felled. There was good feeding here with the young growth of weeds, and the roe loved the cover.

The doe passing through the long avenues of young trees woke blackbirds and hedgesparrows which had nests in the low branches. The trees stood silver, the birds crouched in the black shadows. A hedgesparrow clutching four eggs beneath her thighs saw the hair of the doe's flank a foot away. Her nest of dried moss and deer hair was slung between four brambles. But the doe went on, for the night would not stay on the hill and in the woods for ever, and a deer that has learnt how a bullet can crack open the air about its head knows that daylight must be watched, that tree boles fading into grey sky and the grass showing its leaves must be feared, for the bullets come from the trees, even when the wind is right and shows no hint of fear.

She found a wide grassy ride and dared to run it, for the moon was going through the night and into the west. There was a long shadow on this side, which took her along a hill ridge for nearly a mile. Far below car headlights glimmed upon the hillside now and then and made a little lightening on the bushes.

She came off the ride and along a narrow trackway, where another little moon slid out of the grass in front of the doe and wobbled gently at her feet. Water had collected in a hollow where wheels had puddled out the clay. It was the first watermoon she had seen and she stared, blowing at the reflection to get its scent, smelling the water and then drinking. She went on and the night dew polished her black cleaves again as the clay from the pool was brushed off.

The track went into the wild top of the hill called Bey Hill, and she left the wider way for another path known only to deer that went down into old thorns so thick that a sheep could get tangled. But the deer felt their way by the touch of the twigs on their flanks, and the doe followed the wind again, happy to find that other deer had been that way. She came to a place under yew branches: a kind of small cavern where the low black roof of branches was held up by the yew trunks.

She searched the cavern out, every corner, among the low branches and brittle blackthorn trunks which had died under the yew shade. There was a taste of iron in one place where a coiled iron spike held up fragments of old barbed wire. There was a bottle and a piece of rubber, strange things to be explored. The grove was safe with two small entrances between brambles like tangled wire. She felt warm and lay down to doze in a hollow scraped out in the yew mould by a fallow buck, three weeks before. The moon dropped slowly beyond the thicket roof, and went out.

She woke to black night and a chill wind an hour or two before morning. The yew cavern was on the slope of the hill, and faced the Channel sea; the wind could scorch the yew tops when it was forced up the valley from below.

Rested and alert again, the doe arose and ran back along the deer path. She came through gorse and thorn to a wide place, a hill-top of grass. Here were three mounds on the open top, like rounded clumps of trees. Far away where the moon had gone down was a chain of orange lights that wavered and seemed to crawl along the Channel shore. The wind came up from the valley. She turned down a path that took her off the hill, snatching a few bites of bramble among the woodsage and burnet that grew there. Again she went into the wood and followed currents of the night, avoiding low branches and close-pressed stems of yew trees that formed as deep a thicket as she had not seen before. Often she stopped on her way down through the trees and listened. Scents came all the time, of the new place. There were squirrels, asleep in hollow ash trees and yew twig bowers, a badger somewhere far below. The yew branches over her made gentle sounds with the wind, hiding the rittling of her cleaves in the fragments of dead bark that had fallen from the boughs and trunks. At the bottom of the wood she came to a grassy vale where old yews stood here and there like groups of cattle seen dimly in ancient parklands.

Here in the open she stood a long while in this vale of Kinzerlic, smelling the slow circling of air which had lost the wind and was moving round picking up the scents and smell of everything that was in that quiet, dark place. She smelt the green of fescue grass and the blades of cocksfoot, all asoak with dew and green. She smelt the ash buds breaking, burnet, and the thyme. She fed quickly, moving slowly on along the wood edge, deeper into the valley until she was under the western slope, and there was no wind.

There was an old oak tree and an old yew with one branch broken, another dark place like a cave hidden round by bushes and dogrose, and she lay down as the first light began to come over the hill.

And in that dawn, the wind that had moved her off the hill-top blew again, and came from over the other side of the valley, but now so gentle a wind that the fog that came with the dawn stayed about the hills and valleys, and the wind turned over in slow waves and eddies as it tumbled the fog about. Soon the landscape began to vanish as the fog began to flow. Here and there islands of trees would appear, to be swept away again in the fog-tide, as though the forest were being formed anew. The fog made beads of dew on the longer hairs of the doe's coat, for the glade was moving in the tide, drifting through a screen of vapour droplets. Birds began to sing outside, but they were hidden in the white earth clouds. The doe slept.

In the evening, when the air was warm long after a shadow had moved over the valley from the western slopes, the doe came out from her hiding place. She stood at the wood edge and as she waited there was a movement of dead leaves behind her, and the woodcock flew out from under the oak. For it was night coming, and as by day the spider nets his territory among the grass tops so by night the woodcock draws close the lines of his dominion, above the forest.

The mist came back, but it was a warm mist which gave moisture to the grass. The doe wandered across the valley searching the ground, often standing to listen, eating again quickly.

As the doe fed in the valley of Kinzerlic, pulling over the tips of young ash trees for the cloven buds, she felt the movement within her; the movement that had drawn her all the long night to this place. She turned back to the oak bower, stopping once to let the contraction ease. In a few minutes she was back under the trees, waiting for her young, which would come with the light.

And as the blood rises in the bone cells of a deer's antlers, so the sap is drawn from cell to cell through the outer layer of white wood that is the living tissue of the forest tree. And so that night the buoyant air of spring was drawing northwards the migrating woodland birds: olive-feathered chiff-chaff and willow warbler, nightingale with russet tail, blackcap with the plumage from the pale ash of the winter woodland fires now moss-grown and forgotten, whitethroats with the spider silken-web gorget at their throat, and the shy wood warbler that knew already as it crossed the moon fields of France the beech glade where the yellow morning sun would match its breast. As the woodcock flew, so about the heaths and ferny hills of France nightjars clacked with their wide gape at winter moths under the moon, and flew on, rising singly, in pairs and in dozens as they neared the coast, into the colder higher air until with swallows, shrikes and warblers they formed the lines of force that drew them in a curve across the Channel waters. Flocks of birds arrived that night or in the early dawn, topping white chalk cliffs where the downs ended in the sea in a maelstrom of mist.

They flew into the strange clouds, confused by the

cliff-face eddies of damp air that shrouded their feathers and hurled up the sounds of the sucking tide from far below. They smelt the land and tried to drop to the headland turf glimpsed between the gusts of mist, but the wind drove them up. Others were caught in down-currents and pulled down into the cauldron of sea-fog. They recovered and were carried forward over the white foam, then suddenly up, up, past the stratas of ancient chalk rock, past gulls crouched on ledges waiting for a bird to dash itself against the cliff, past the cliff-face rabbits that hopped among chalk pinnacles like mountain goats, past the frieze of grass and blowing grains of earth of the cliff top and up into the cloud. Some fluttered into the ledges and crouched there for several hours. Many were hurled inland and dived into the wind-torn thorn hedges that were moulded upon the slopes of the down.

Later, in the afternoon, the birds felt the warmth of the sun and rested, then flew north on their journey of the spring, feeling safe that the long sea crossing was behind. Many stopped for several days in garden or orchard, and sang unexpectedly with blackbird and thrush at the first sign of dawn. Nightingales sang in small suburban gardens and then passed on and were soon singing fifty miles away.

Many hundreds of the travelling birds were heading for the forest. Some already had nested there, while others had hatched there the year before and were following in the closing stages of migration the only pattern of countryside which they knew. The shape of rivers which they remembered, the outline of lakes which they had seen but once, the coloured patterns of towns and cities, each bird knew and followed with growing anticipation and excitement as hedge and field slipped by beneath them.

In the days after this, at dusk or at noontime, by spring winds or in the sudden warmth of early sundays, the migrants flew into the yew forest around the valley of Kinzerlic, which the doe had found. The wood warblers came to the glade as the first bud sheaths opened. Chiff-chaffs had forged the metal of their song in the cold days of March; now they hammered the notes from the high branches of oak and ash as though claiming the whole forest with the stormcock. White-throats made every bramble bed their own. Their song crackled in the air as they flew upwards and back in a ragged arc. They were the birds of heat; their song would spark through every heat-shimmering day. Into the most dense of the bramble beds came a grasshopper warbler. In the still nights of early May it sat for hours low among the brambles and reeled out its song and spun its silver web of sound, that formed patterns like a spider's web until it caught a hen bird, passing a hundred yards away. Then together the two barred and speckled birds crept deep among the brambles finding their joy in the secret places where only mice and beetles rustled the leaves.

Over the forest swallows dipped, sometimes singing while they took insects rising out of the oaks and the chestnut coppice, and with them came a cuckoo, fluttering like a spent arrow—hawk-like body, sharp wings and tail, yet without the sinew and purpose of a hawk.

In the darkness after these warm spring days the air cooled, then moistened, and received into itself again all the scents of new growth: sweet briar, nettle sap, young birch leaves, wild garlic and the banks of green growing into summer grasses. When the air was still, every tree was enlarged by its own scent. From the balsam poplar scent tumbled, heavy as sap, from the soft leaves and drifted through the glades for a great distance.

In these secret nights, when the stars glided through the trees and turned silently about their Pole, as Jupiter moved down the northern sky to lay heavy with earth mist and when Venus commanded the night with its silver light, like a small moon within the northern colours of the forgotten sun, then the nightingales came to the forest. They searched the places for the birch and hazel trees, the nettles and the brambles; the places where the oak leaves were thick which they would use for nest building, and the glades which they would shake with song. Nettle sap hung like smoke on the air. They tasted, and fell down among the stems, and song bubbled to join the night scents. They crept lower, searched deep into the green, feeling it hold their bodies as green waves had enclosed many that had tried to cross the sea on migration. All night the nightingales and warblers fluttered down into the forest like spent leaves of the migration flood. Olive and brown, grey, black and green: tired, but with the joy of return bubbling suddenly into song at dawn, and before. Song and scent lay heavy on the night air now that the deadening north winds had gone. The southern air drift brought old scents of their winter homes, of desert and olive grove, which they knew. The nightingales sang down the moonbeams deep in the hawthorn thickets.

Chapter Two

In those May days many creatures saw the new-born buck while he lay under the oak tree. A great tit which had a nest in the oak peered at him, edging round from branch to twig and then clinging upside down on the trunk, the better to see. The kid lay very still, only the nostrils of his small black nose moving all the time. '*Quink,*' cried the bird seeing the movement, giving an alarm to its mate sitting on eggs in a cleft of the oak. Soon it was used to the small brown animal curled asleep with a sun pattern across his back, which did not move even when the sun swung through the southern sky into evening. For Capreol knew that he must never move. A squirrel which had been there when the kid was born but had since forgotten, jerked its tail and gave a mild curse through its yellow front teeth, thinking from his curled form that the kid might be a fox. The sound called a blackbird into the oak: it hopped here and there looking for the domed silhouette of an owl which it thought the squirrel might be mobbing. The blackbird saw nothing and flew away, but a crow which had a nest, a witch's broom of twigs hidden in the smoke of dense yew leaves, came to see what was happening. It saw the kid and hopped down through the branches, looking carefully around and then stopping on the lowest branch, peering with slow side-turnings of its head. Its mantle bristled; it was not sure. Twice it nearly fell as it stopped itself from dropping to the ground. A long while ago it had found a leveret in the wood and had feasted for two days after dapping its soft skull. But the kid was larger, and the crow went back to the wood.

The kid was tired with his efforts to suckle when the doe's full udders drew her to him. He slept in between, unaware of the birds moving about in the tree above—even when a wood pigeon landed with slapping of stiff pinions on leaves. The wood dove trod the flat branches which were soft with moss, and it thought of the twig nest there which would hold its two white eggs, and its call was deep away, far, in the down woods.

In the evening the doe slipt to the kid through narrow tracks that would scarcely show the passing of a hare in the grass and between the bushes. He struggled up to meet her and her tongue quickly washed his eyes and smoothed back his coat, rubbing off cobwebs and dust from his leaf nest. His legs splayed out to hold the little body up, and his head was raised to her teat. She looked about and listened to everything that moved in that quiet place where night came so soon: already it was dark under the oak. She heard the heaving of moles in the grass roots, the mutter of a crow, cough of a fallow buck up the valley, scritch of a mouse and fan of the white owl over. Her head moved quickly to each sound as she balanced to the kid's butting, and sometimes she was thrown a little off-balance and her legs carefully readjusted without sound in the dead leaves.

After ten minutes he had fed enough and she took him out into the starlight. She fed on oak buds and the tips of a heather bush. Often she turned around and held her muzzle to him to ensure that he was close to her. She went no farther than the edges of the oak, for he was too small to walk more than a few steps at a time. Then she made him lie down between two antheaps, which hid him, and grazed a little for grass and herbs. There was cocksfoot and brome, and the narrow leaves of fescue, and she snatched some flower heads of ground ivy and the birdseye speedwell whose petals in the daytime had been the colour of a fine clear air sometimes seen over the sea coast. Often she jerked up her head to stare into the night, ears swivelling to each sound.

The next day on the fields of Strakedown a scare gun was set up to keep pigeons off the kale. The doe hated its sudden tunnelling of sound round the valley, like a circle of thunder. In the dark, when she was feeding, her target would flare out white, the tail-warning of a chased animal. At night they rested in the meadow where wild parsnip plants were growing, and became soaked with dew. Capreol lay next to his mother, and felt the warmth coming from her body. In the dawn they went back to the oak and its long branches that were held out to hide them again in leaf-twilight. There the doe looked around, nibbling a leaf or two but watching the forms of antheaps and grass tussocks and small hawthorn bushes fading away from the night. She was very beautiful then, for the sun, far down beyond the hill of Strakedown, had made the sky white and she was a honey-gold. By her side Capreol was no larger than a hare, but with even finer legs.

The sun rose, the deer drew under the tree, and only

their hocks caught the light and showed them to a watcher walking in the woodland enclave of the vale of Kinzerlic. He moved quietly away, knowing what it meant. Then those eight points of light faded, for deer must hide from the sun, and day is an enemy.

Capreol lay resting there soon after daylight, when a rustling in the dry leaves made him alert, though he did not move. It was a rat. It circled Capreol, lifting on hind legs to find the scent, and, being uncertain of what it found, sat back and washed its face.

Blue scars showed on the hump of its back where a ferret had almost scratched its life away, in a narrow tunnel in the chalk, a dark February ago. The rat had saved itself by keeping quite still and so protecting its neck and throat. Now it did not come any closer but picked up a dead bramble leaf in its mouth and ran back hurriedly through the oak leaves, for it was a doe, and it felt the old movements within its womb, and its nest was yet half made. The rat had half circled the deer, but had never given it any scent, and Capreol soon forgot.

The oak tree's shadow slid as Capreol slept, and he awoke to hot patches of sun on his body, a sun which had travelled halfway across the glade when he woke again. In the afternoon a queen bumble-bee tumbled into the cage of sunlight, bemused by the barring of gold and black everywhere. She sank with a low drone on to an oak leaf an inch from Capreol's muzzle, and there sunbathed. Capreol lay still. When the doubloon of sun had moved on, the queen felt cold, for she was tired, having imbibed little nectar since daybreak. Upon the gauzy eyes and shiny black shield of her head were strange green growths like minute snakes' heads, lying tangled about. The queen rubbed at them feebly with her forelegs, as she had scratched and scraped for most of the day. Capreol did not like the black leg waving near to his muzzle and drew back. The snakes' heads, each no thicker than a thread, were glued to the queen's forehead and half covered the eyes. Flight had been difficult, making her hit the oak leaves when she had been searching for hawthorn flowers near by. The snakes' heads were the male parts of an orchid that grew outside the wood on the banks around the old war-time tracks. The queen had seen the purple flowers and followed the flight path of purple spots which the flower displayed in its lips. She had landed there and thrust for nectar, pressing into the flower's body and, drawing out, had dragged away the stalk of male pollen. Moving thus from flower to flower, the queen had taken on a score of stalks, pollinating flower by flower in her eager thrust for nectar in the soft flowers' wombs which waited on the touch of pollen.

Now she was exhausted by the grappled head of wilting stalks that she could not remove. Soon she tried to fly again, feeling a desire to return to the moss nest under the root of a yew tree. She crept forward, shimmering with a wing-whine which was all her last strength frazzling away. Capreol jumped up as the bee touched his leg and at the sudden movement the bumble-bee lay back, holding one black leg into the air to ward off an attack.

The warm days of May brought more birds to the valley, and they moved unseen among oak leaves that were opening out, shaking down patterns of song that could be heard long after the birds had gone on. Outside, the daylight turned gradually to the green mist of the seabed. Then blossoms opened, and the may was a clotting of white, shining through on Capreol. From the ground, unfurling bracken broke with downbent head, arched and downy with scorched hairs like the curled neck of the new-born buck.

All this he saw, but kept still, as he knew he must not move.

One morning the kid was greatly alarmed by a strange, brilliant creature that landed on a bough above him. It was a golden pheasant, one of several that had been reared and then released in the woods. In spring dawns when the owl hunted and men were not about, the golden pheasant left its yew bower where it awaited the first lighting of the sky and, dropping with cascade of feathers into the gloom, walked here and there, stopping for the old hawthorn peggles that lay about. Always it walked to a certain old yew broken on one side. Now it arose with a screech and alighted on a long snake of a branch shorn of twigs above the little buck. Here it paraded, raising yellow mantle, fanning barred tail, awaiting the calls of its rivals. But it had none, for it was a bird alone; and when branches and twigs, wet with night mist, began to shine with red and gold colours the cock screeked its threats at the rising sun.

On another day the kid smelt a multitude of dark scents that came suddenly and hung about the brambles. He did not move, even though the scents made his guts begin to freeze. There were shuffling noises, noises of the grass moving roughly, not as when the doe came quietly; noises of the grass torn by heavy feet. But he did not move. Then there were other noises, throat sounds, and a cough. Once there was a sharp click, which made the small target of hair now tucked into the dead leaves move and rise with fear. But his eyes slept, and the movement of his nose breathing was no more than that of a beetle pushing up a leaf.

Outside in the narrow glade was a man in grey. The man waited by the yew tree, hoping to shoot a crow which had a nest somewhere in the wood, waiting for it to return. Behind the screen of dark foliage he heard the crows talking, *knok, knok,* soft as a raven's whisper. They were working towards the nest, but were afraid to pass a gap in the wood. The grey man stared into the ever-greens but saw nothing, no movement, only the soft croaks that seemed to come from farther away. For a long while he stood there, knowing the hen bird would become desperate. When she did slip in flight across the gap, gliding swiftly with wings half closed with gathered speed, he was ready and snapped a shot that cut a path of yew twigs behind her tail. A few pigeons clapped out of the trees and circled high over the wood. Two gunshots off, the cock bird cried as though shot, leaping like a dolphin from the green sea of yew, diving away at once. Under the oak the kid clung to the earth, which was his day-mother. Squirrels chattered and screamed for a while. The pigeons which had been frightened out of their nests circled and glided back into the trees. It was quiet again. Now the kid heard other crow calls: *krak krak* – hardly audible, coming from here and there under the green sea. In the silence, as birds and animals began to move and call, the grey man saw the crows once only over a gunshot distant. Then there was half an hour of silence from the crows and the grey man began to think of moving on. He thought that perhaps the crow had not yet begun to sit tight. He would creep to the nest and wait under it before dawn on the following day. As he was turning to leave, his eye caught the crow flying up out of the tree a hundred yards away. He stood still, watching the bird fly up with ragged wing strokes until it was high over the trees. It appeared to the grey man that the crow was flying away, but suddenly it rolled in the air and dived down at him. With its wings closed it was a dart, fine barbed, black: the grey man raised his gun and fired before the gun was at his shoulder. The bird did not flinch: the long swing down from that height was unaltered, and it came on at his head until suddenly sweeping up again at the last moment, and the grey man felt the end of the swing strike at his heart. He stood still, then felt sudden distaste for the place, for the darkness under the yews that was deeper than shade. It was a chill of the air that the dark trees imparted, a poisoned air. But when he strode away into the open the strokes of the sun pierced the coldness of his body like spikes of glass. He did not feel warm again until he had reached his home.

Quietly the kid lay, become again part of the earth. The air seemed quiet, but the sound of the shot had gone round the valley and into the ground, and there he picked out its last reverberations. The doe came from island to island of the trees and bushes, risking daylight, harbouring under each for a moment until she reached him. When she led him out he smelt the grass fouled by what he had not known before as harmful, and he remembered the smells of human and dog, grease from boots, and the choking scent of nitro powder lying in the grass.

Later they found a place in the bramble, where a hare had crawled once to her young, in the spring, making a low tunnel. The brambles grew round a hottentot head of roots pulled out behind a fallen yew. Round about other yews had been left fractured by snow and gales or by the weight of their own branches. Many younger trees had fallen even before their time, losing their grip on the thin soil when heavy rains caused the ground to slide on the steep slopes. The trees heaved up a mat of soil on the roots and flints that were impounded between the wood. On a tree which had fallen one May when it rained every day, a sharp flint of unusual shape stuck out, making a perch for blackbirds. The flint had been buried for more than two thousand years, until the yew tree's roots had gripped it in the chalk. It was two-sided, with a smooth curve brought to an edge. The flint held the edge which had been worn to it once, those years ago. The tree had fallen in the glade around the badger's sett, where nettles and elders grew. It was a gully in the steep side of the hill, where the yew trees grew very thick and where the air was always still under the hill, and smoking with the fog drift after rain.

One calm night there was a crack and a small rustle-rumble from the old grove across the valley on the hill, and enough earth-bump to set one or two pheasant cocks crowing. A branch as thick as a man's chest had dropped from a yew, the wood at the fracture broken into scallops and lumps that showed no lines or sinews; petrified by rot. Half the heart of the yew had been pulled out, revealing a deep well within the tree, filled with a cake of black rubbish that had fallen in through small holes and cracks throughout the years. There were over a score of starlings' nests buried in that tree, some with remains of blue eggs when the birds had quarrelled. There was the skeleton of a young squirrel and dead fleas left behind by the starlings when the gaps above had closed up with trunk growth of internal roots.

Soon afterwards a white owl found the tree and dropped down into the black hollow like a falling shuttlecock and explored the cavern; then he stood at the entrance and cast a pellet of mouse fur.

In the afternoon rabbits came from their burrows around the badger holes and played on the pad of earth thrown up from deep below, that was still warm from the morning sun. There were bones there, a badger's shoulder-blade two hundred years old and a human jaw with two white teeth ground flat. Capreol watched the rabbits going farther out to the grass bank beyond the trees as the hill shadow went up the other side of the valley. Sometimes they ran back with black eyes staring at sounds of people far away or earth-bumps from horses on the hill above. Then they appeared again, and a buck rabbit with an old ear wound came up to him, reaching forward with nose quivering for scent. Capreol stretched for play and kicked out his forefeet and ran round the rabbit, frightening it up into the wood.

In a while, when the rabbits came up again and were

out on the bank for the first dew, bobbing about after each other or sitting still, holding spears of grass in their mouths when they listened through the earth to people walking in the valley, or to mouse squeaks, or to a pigeon flap in the trees above, or to nothing, and when the deer were beginning to feed on anything that was in reach, then a black nose like a bit of beach coal appeared from one of the badger holes. It was an old boar badger who had tunnelled the chalk hill for thirteen years, either in this sett or another one two miles away in a place above Windens called Barrowdown Bottom where there was a pocket of sand. Behind him four cubs pushed and bit like polecat ferrets. The boar ambled out and listened to the last noise of the day, letting out a belch that was the remains of five young field voles, twenty-four lobworms, and some old acorns. Every hill path was known to him through the bramble tops on the hill and the yew thickets where lobworms coiled and slipped slowly like intestines of the earth and the grass dells where craneflies danced in September. He explored the fields, marking year after year what was planted and knowing when it could be harvested, whether wheat or the milk of green sap-barley, turnip roots or cattle cake laid for fattening bullocks.

On a dark night once when snow was laying he had found two pheasants wounded by shooting and eaten both, with every tail feather, and afterwards he had slept for a week. In spring he dug orchid tubers before the purple flowers were budded from the ground, or scratched voles out from their grass runs. Once a mother rat had bit his lip and hung there in a frenzy for her young as he swung her back and forth unable to catch her in his mouth and break her back that was blue-scarred in a ferret fight. He had left the rat, but little else had ever bested him. Running into the gloom on his night prowl of the hill he avoided the deer, not wanting the sideways kick of their legs. In darkness enough to show half a dozen stars like glints of glass specks, the deer fed with the rabbits on sweet stems of fescue on the edge of the glade, while the badger cubs snarled and bit each other in play over the man's jawbone, somewhere under the black yews.

Chapter Three

Past midsummer by a few days, and on the old heath on Bey Hill summer left this spring for ever. The deer found a grassy glade under an old hawthorn, surrounded all about by brambles. The hawthorn had once been there alone, the only tree at the highest point of the hill, bent almost double by the seawind. Sheep had once rubbed its bark shiny brown. Its bark now was dusty with algae and lichens, and its trunk had tried to straighten itself as other hawthorn sprang up round about. There were holes like old canker marks in the bark: several rifle bullets were embedded in the wood. It was a tree formed of wars and wind, but its marks had healed, and unlike the others it had grown thick clusters of spines in defence of itself.

Its blossom was heavier, too, for it had become indrawn and no longer sent out long green sappy twig shoots, but formed a domed crown; conserved itself for other wars. The shade beneath this tree was almost as the yews', and the deer liked it for this.

When the other hawthorns had shed their last white petals and were forming berries like little apples, this old hawthorn held on to its flowers, which were guarded by thick spines and leaves. At last it shed them, and as the last flowers began to fall white flowers of blackberry opened, creased like the wings of ghost-swift moths which were then emerging in the night.

Outside, beyond, the days seemed calm and still. Grasses on the Downs had begun to turn colour. Birds no longer sang after the dew had gone. Summer swarmed with heat and the unseen movements of a crowding life behind the grasses and the leaves. The deer see what perhaps is never seen by men: a shrew, fly eggs clustered on a bloody nose-tip; a single fly arcing out from a gap in the trees, tangling its black curving thread of flight back into the insect-whirring madness; a deer's brown flank, at first thought to be sunlight, splashing on to hawthorn leaves. These perhaps are seen; and sometimes too it is the deer who are unaware of being watched.

The watcher saw the doe, although she did not know it. She was thirsty, and was on the way to some rusty, filthy water in the fire water tanks, speckled with pigeon quill scurf and the floating jelly of a drowned whitethroat coated with a mucus of fungus. She had drunk there before, her neck deeply arched over the rim, tongue just reaching the surface of the water.

So the hawthorn held its flowers and made a denser shade to protect its roots.

One day when Capreol and his mother lay sleeping they were woken by the gentle rustle and uncertain padding of a rabbit moving through the undergrowth.

The rabbit was very near. Outside the hot day was brilliant, in early afternoon. The rabbit came closer, touching every bramble stem, sometimes feeling with its nose along low branches. It was over a hundred yards from its burrow yet it was unalarmed at the daylight. Its eyes were slits of pus, and day and night were one.

Capreol watched as the animal shambled nearly to his nose, then he started with a sudden fear just before they touched. At this the rabbit leaped sideways and hit a yew trunk and fell back in confusion. There it squatted, shaking a little, its head half-raised, trying to untangle the source of danger through organs made useless by disease. Its backbone stood out like that of an old dog. Its fur was dull and matted here and there with mud splashes. Its nose festered with running sores and mucus. It was the first rabbit that year to contract the plague of myxomatosis, injected through the proboscis of a flea that had waited six months in the dank cavern of an old warren on the hill.

It ran off, at first with a kind of creeping run, then jumping with erratic leaps, fearing everything, pursued by the sounds of its own tangled leaps in the brambles. At evening, when the deer came out again to feed, there were rabbits all along the edges of the woods, playing there, chasing one another. . . .

When the green-awned barley began to show the movement of winds across the gentle-sloping fields, then summer had come to the Downs. In a week of sun the barley awns were bleached purple at the tips.

Summer brought two game birds, smaller than partridges, to the barley fields. Day after day they hid among the stalks, finding insects and seeds of chickweed, corn spurrey, and birdseye speedwell. In the mornings they would dust in the dry chalk silt of the bridle path which had run from the sunken trackways in the winter. They would creep back into the corn, slipping between the stems, small enough to walk between the drills without even shaking the dew from leaf blades. They were quails, and they had paired before their migration among the juniper bushes of the Mediterranean coast.

The dusty tracks, the steely sky and the infinite haven of the barley brought a bubble of joy to the cock bird's throat: *quit quit-quit,* liquid triple note. Song of old cornfields, with the call of pee-wit and song of skylark.

Summer brought, too, the tall grasses in the old places. At midsummer they opened their green, dense flowers which had risen soft and formless in the spring, sheathed secretly in folded blades. Now the anthers hung out awaiting the mating of the wind: purple of cocksfoot, yellow of brome, white of oat grass. One evening the grey man saw, in the thin alto-stratus cloud to the west, two patches of rainbow colour, one each side of the sun. 'Sundogs,' he said aloud, and was happy, for he knew it to be a sign of a long dry summer.

And summer brought the flies. One morning the doe led her kid from the valley of Kinzerlic in those days after midsummer. The wind from the north had dropped. Clouds came from the north-west, slowly, not seeming to move. Clouds like the cobwebs that hang in barns, a netting of high grey vapour. The plain below Kinzerlic seemed to smoulder with the oily fumes of fire damp. The grasses were taller than Capreol and darkened his flanks with dew. Flies came from the bushes and buzzed about his eyes, falling into his coat in their eagerness. The doe sought the hill and the cooler air. They left foyle slots in the rock roses growing over antheaps and they leapt the fence into the hill plantation, finding a deep cool among the pines. Pine needles matted the ground, making a soft bed. The kid licked at a last low-whirring fly that had followed them under the trees, and was lost now in this cool shade. The fly droned up uncertainly to the light and Capreol dozed. His long ears drooped, eyes closed, and black muzzle settled on to the pine needles.

But the doe stayed awake. She heard the hollow ring of horses' hooves coming all the way through the arch of chalk bedrock, which formed Bey Hill, as riders came up the bridle paths and trotted around the forest. She heard people talking a long way off, but these were background noises, as were the songs of birds. Only when voices of a walking group, passing within fifty yards, were raised in laughter did her head jerk around to the sound. Then she stared in that direction long after the people had walked on down the hill. She dozed, but woke abruptly when a pheasant shook itself in a dust bath, twenty yards away. The pheasant, a large pale cock bird, a bohemian, with spurs showing his three long and hard seasons among the poachers and dogs of Kinzerlic, was content. The days of spring lust were over, the seven hen birds he commanded were sitting on second broods of eggs or leading chicks in the long grass; he had begun to lose track of them. Since daybreak he had gorged on wild strawberries and made his crop full as the sun changed from pink to gold. Then he had settled into the fine dusty earth of an old antheap which had become extinct when the pines shaded out heath plants. There he had lazed, kicking first on one side, then the other. Dust drifted into yellow sunbeams, the pheasant's wattles glowed, old moult feathers were shaken out of tail and wing. It became a shapeless thing, covered with dry earth, only its eye, moving continually over the scene around, gave it life at all. Then it had stood up, and with a mighty thudding of wings, shaken a fine silt of dust over half a dozen yards.

When this had woken the doe, she found that flies had penetrated the gloom. There was no breeze. The plain far below Bey Hill had become grey with heat fog.

The doe knew that away from the woods the flies would be less trouble. When they had begun to make her flank ripple in irritation and when the kid shook his head violently, not having yet learnt the slow rhythmic head nod which keeps flies from settling, she moved out of the wood and into the open, down to a field of barley. Flies would not settle near corn. But cornfields are open, and the roe are lovers of shadow, broken sunlight patterns, leaves, bramble fronds, the secret winding paths which only the roe can easily follow, for the paths close up behind them. But they moved, and crossing the open turf came to a sheep fence. The fence was topped by one strand of barbed wire. Normally the doe would clear this, a standing jump, even though the wire was level with the tops of her ears. But she had the kid. She ran down the wire, but the mesh seemed too small; then she found that the bottom mesh was a little larger, larger than her head. She knelt, pushed her head through, and scrambled under on her belly. The kid came after her, and they waded into the barley a few steps, and settled, completely hidden. But the sky was open.

By night they left the cornfield and scrambled through the fence, wandering back into Kinzerlic to browse on dogwood, hawthorn, and the hard little leaves of yew. At dawn they returned to the cornfields. It was their home for a few days. Sometimes horse-riders passed close by on the path on their way through to the woods at West Holte, but the deer could not be seen in the corn.

On hot days in summer when the heat rose like bubbles of blown glass to scorch the slopes of the Downs, the swifts would leave the eaves and tiles of the old city and wheel and tumble like specks of ash in the summer fire. High up in the haze insects were travelling on migration and the swifts pursued them, their thin screaming cries lost to the land below.

Sometimes a pair of birds faster even than the swifts would fall like two blue blades out of the sky, curving down into the swifts and taking one of them before swinging back into the empty air above. The birds were hobbys, relatives of the peregrine that now were birds almost of myth in the South and which had bred once on the chalk cliffs.

High over the valley the hobby lay balancing into the bubble of heat, and as the scents of hay and the thin dust of the distant city flowed gently up from the plain, the male hobby bent head beneath body and tore at the thin sinewy carcase until the cleaving pinions of the swift spun away.

The hobbys had nested in a clump of pines on a heath five miles distant; the vale of Kinzerlic was a ten-minute glide and flicker of wings away, soaring on summer currents to the spine of the downs. The hobbys came to the vale of yews when the air flowed gently up from the plain to the south, for then they could ride the currents, swinging back and forth over the whole valley like boats anchored on a running chain. As they drifted, they watched the ground.

Dark green fritillary butterflies were emerging from the cocoons suspended under dog violet leaves. Climbing up grass stems with furled wings, they waited as their wings opened and dried. High above, the hobbys waited and watched the mouse-like creepings of the butterflies, saw the colours open, set, tremble before that first flight; the blink of orange in the grass, the sudden jagged dart away; sparks of summer energy. The hobbys fell and knocked away a swathe of grass pollen before catching a butterfly. Swooping straight back to their pitch, they fed, head tucked down to talon, until the butterfly wings were cast away and spun far beyond the top of the hill into the still air of the north face. By nightfall, on these days of southern wind, a score of wings lay on the moss and leaves.

All summer the swifts played on the hilltop air, and the hobbys were with them, facing whatever funnelling of air came each day. In a south-west wind they hung above grey Channel waters which were white-chipped by small waves, and on this wind they could soar without a wing movement for this was the wind of the great valley, a wind funnel that would have thrown a peregrine a thousand feet into the air.

Then, when the north-west wind followed, the hobbys were joined by kestrels that would soar on the northern face of Bey Hill, which looked out across the downland hills and the beech forest of Riallhart, and here the kestrels slid in and out of cloud shadows with a change of plumage colours from black to brick pink and the thunder-cloud grey of the cock kestrel's mantle. Notched with yellow was his beak then, like the little tormentil flowers opening on the hill heath below him.

When he was two months old, Capreol couched on the hill among the gorse bushes. Above, close-pressed within her feathers, the hobby slid into a rise of air pouring over the hill-top. All day she swung here and there above Capreol, who observed the short head and sharp wings that cut the sky about until this safe clear dome was hair-cracked near to breaking. At last it was evening and the hobby went, and Capreol rose stiffly again to the safety of stars.

Another day Capreol lay beneath a thorn bush and the dark cross was seen through the leaves moving back and forth, crossing from one way or another. Gradually he became used to the little falcon, giving it no more attention than the swifts which beat over him leaving a dry scudder of sound from their wings.

One night the doe and Capreol went into the valley, and there was another deer standing in the glade near to the place where Capreol had been born. It stayed in a dark opening in the wood, its antlers reaching the young yew boughs above. The doe watched, not moving, while a buzzard crossed the sky in circles uncoiling westwards. She went towards the deer, and Capreol kept close to her. But the figure had gone.

Through the days of summer people came to walk on the hill, and children's voices shrilled in the valley. Many brought dogs, letting them run loose on wild scenting trails. There was a dalmatian one day that galloped into the wood while its owner walked heedlessly on. The dog was happy at its freedom for it spent all its days in the upstairs of a house in the nearby city, sucking with its nose at the scent of a cat that slept a few inches on the

other side of the closed and locked door. Every other day its owner brought the dog, whose limbs were lithe and strong as a deer's, to exercise, before the return to its prison. The dalmatian found a young hare and chased it round the antheaps and hillocks of a quiet grassy glade till the hare broke a leg landing awkwardly in a hollow, and the dog's owner, a quarter of a mile away, hearing thin far-off screams, thought of wild nature's ways.

The dog smelt the two deer a hundred yards away and worked quietly up to them. They heard the quiet padding coming closer, the fearful sounds of daytime that meant an enemy, man or dog. The animal circled their tent of brambles but before it reached the opening the deer ran. Capreol followed his mother and they were into the shelter of the next yew tree before the dalmatian found the scent, for it was dulled by confinement. Then it set on to their trail and the doe went as fast as her kid could follow, bursting bramble fronds for him with her great leaps, turning always to see that he was still at her back. They galloped through a little grove of ash saplings, making them clack together; they frightened the brown owl from his perch in the thicket, and landed almost on top of two people asleep in the sun, who sat upright and pointed; but the deer did not notice them. The dog was twenty yards away, running in erratic side-searching for the track, yet keeping up. The doe took the kid into the wood, hoping the darkness of the branch cage would hide them as it always had but fearful that her young one would not be able to race up the hill as she could. She turned to him to let him catch up, seeing the dog's coat below flickering through sunshafts. Near the top of the hill they passed a woman, who shouted and threw her stick at the dog, but it took no notice.

Capreol lagged and the doe turned to him, seeing that he was done. In the wild heather tops of the hill she plunged down into a bramble tunnel where pheasants crept in times of danger, and the kid crawled after her his tongue white with foam. They crawled on their bellies for a hundred yards, and the doe's face was torn with fine threads and cobwebs of blood by the brambles. The dalmatian had no courage for the spiny place and did not follow. The deer came into an open place and Capreol lay on the ground, sides heaving, but got up at last and swayed at the doe's side. So they stood listening, while the sun wrinkled the sea ten miles away and tiny speckled packs of white sails showed a race was in progress in the harbour.

An hour later the man, who had enjoyed the hill and the summer air and had watched the changing patterns of light across the valley, felt with gratitude the wet press of his dalmatian's nose in his palm as he waited near his car.

The deer found a glade in the hilltop plantation where some young beech trees had been killed by a black fallow buck four years ago, for this had been his rutting stand. Capreol folded into the tall seeded grass without making any couch. His eyes drooped and closed as his muzzle rested in the grass. The doe stayed alert but there was nothing any more to disturb them. There was, among the pines, the smell of old heathland as resin sweated on young buds and out of blueing scars from the brashings. Once Capreol woke with a memory of the chase-fear but the dog vanished as his eyes opened. Tortoiseshell butterflies were gliding across the glade, seen only as wedges disappearing and returning from the shadows. Once the wing of a fritillary fell into the glade and fixed on a grass blade near him. High above the hobby falcon fell over the sky like a flung anchor. He slept again, but woke often as the hound drew up in dark memory. Small clouds came, and made a dimming, and went. Sweat flies found them, searching feverishly in their coats and over their ears and muzzles. It became very hot. The butterflies came down into the grass. A turtle dove landed with gentle flacking of wings among the pine needles; it shook a cropful of mash-feed into the craws of its two young, whose feathers were sheathed with blue membrane like the pine shoots.

In the evening clouds like long goose quills hardly moved across the sky, making the sun into a white opal.

The barley had turned gold in a week. Corn buntings came into song, the last birds of summer. They sat on the barbed-wire fences and felt the heat from the cornfields, and their song was the song of the everlasting summer, and the poppies in the corn, and the scabious flowers which were pale blue, and the white dusty tracks that led up to the horizon.

The roe loved the cooling of the night, and leaped down into the valley. Sometimes the doe played chasing games with her kid in the long grasses, running in an enclave in the valley between the yew and the oaks, near to the place where the kid was born. They chased round and round and made two circles, a figure of eight, that crossed the paths of hares and voles and was known only to themselves, for the long grasses swayed back behind them. The game lasted sometimes for a few minutes, sometimes for an hour. The carrion crow saw them and circled in curiosity. One night they had been seen by the watcher hiding in a tall oak, lying unseen within the boughs. He had watched the circles of hissing grass converge and separate and the head of the doe sometimes breast the green surf of the grassy meadow like a sea horse, until the darkness came and the owl of the hollow yew landed near him inside the leafy shelter. The man had watched with night glasses and had seen, as he was about to leave, another track of moving grass stems, grey in the heat of the summer night, moving towards the play ring doublings beneath him, and as he watched there was a shape like a crooked dagger amongst the swirling grass.

Chapter Four

Summer was hardening, day by day. A grey sky, scorched earth, brazen cornfields: summer was unquenched.

On the hills the grasses became flaxen. They had shed their seeds, and were the empty husks that would stand like corn till the snow laid them into the earth again. Day after day thunder flies rose from flowers of hawkbit, where they had lived their lives in the little golden sun-flowers of the hills. The hawkbit turned grey, the tiny scorpion-bodied flies drifted on the airs to a new life, many miles away. Men spoke of rain, as the thunder flies settled on their brown arms and necks; they looked into the sky, felt the wind moving lightly from one side or another, never a certain quarter, for an anticyclone covered the land from the Azores to the Northern Lights. By day small clouds of dust arose from cornfields, as the first fields were cut. By night the combine-harvesters droned on when all else was quiet, behind headlight beams that stalked up and down to the dawn.

The deer were greatly troubled by flies, even in the corn, and they moved restlessly from place to place. The barley heads bent double on their stalks, the cornfields seethed white with heat, like surf. Evening after evening the sundogs guarded the sky. And in the shadow which folded the vale of Kinzerlic into the night, bringing dew and the sweet scents of honeysuckle, the roe deer came out into the glade between the yew trees, like wood elves.

For five nights the doe and her kid ran together, by day they slept. They had returned to the little tree clump of yew and oak where the kid had been born and lay for those first days, among the rising rose-bay stems. The memory of the dalmatian dog made the doe at first uneasy, for deer live by their experiences, and are able to pass fear on to the next generation. The fallow of Petwood Park, it was said by the Keeper, feared landrovers long after the stalker there, who had driven one to get close enough to shoot, had passed on.

They circled the grove, peering into the shadows. Capreol remembered the trees and leapt the bramble barrier, slid through the spindle thicket and dodged low under the yew boughs to the bed of yew needles where he had curled up for so many days.

One evening Capreol saw the old buck. He was bending a young oak and scraping the bark right down to the cambium with the pearls of his coronet. Capreol saw the buck scrape at an antheap, scattering dozens of ants. The kid came to his mother and butted her teat; but she ran away among the wild parsnips. Soon she came back to him, and led him across the glade to a dewberry bush, where they browsed. But she was restless and jerked her head up every few seconds to listen and stare around the glade, the dewberry leaves half chewed in her mouth.

Later the buck came to the doe and butted her flank. She ran again into the forest of wild parsnips and trotted a pattern known to the roe for thousands of years and the buck followed the encircling path that would bind them. Capreol saw them now and then, saw her pale target vanish or her head appear, and the antlers of the buck moving through the parsnip stems, and he knew he must be alone for a while.

As the deer ran, hoverflies which had been sipping at the yellow umbel flowers by day were shaken off the wild parsnips and droned away. Some came and settled on the flowers around the kid, near the group of young oaks where he lay.

Gentle and quiet are the hoverflies, wasp-striped, but not in offence like the wasp; sippers of nectar like the butterflies. Gold and black bars hid their bodies in the glade of the woodland, where they rocked with invisible wings in shafts of sunlight. In the plantations, where the kid had spent so many days of summer, they had sometimes landed on his flank, a touch so light, unfelt: not the crawling feverish searching of the sweat flies but still, still, there to look with bland brown eyes, bodies moving as with the rhythm of breathing. Even as the kid blinked, they would be gone, hanging above him again; seed parachutes of rosebay moving through the glades could not move more lightly.

Now two or three settled on his flank, and he did not know they were there until he felt one spring faintly off his fur. Memory of the sweat flies made him run his tongue at them.

On the first day of August, two hours after the sun had risen, a heat settled in the valley between the hilltops like fog. The deer sheltered in the damp grasses under the oaks and lay quiet. By noon the sun was brown-gold under the trees; the air was a smoked glass. Swifts were going south, looking no more than a cloud of midges high above, a summer going that no one in that valley saw.

A few minutes past the noon hour a small glinting wing from an insect fell on Capreol's hair. For an hour it beamed a tiny light back and forth as he breathed. It was the wing of an ant, which had fallen from five hundred feet after the passing of the swifts. From grassy mounds all in the valley, ants were swarming and taking flight. Thus it had happened every first August day of heat: so it always would. Capreol was startled by the black and brown bodies which would not fly away when he darted his tongue into the midst of them. They dribbled from holes in an antheap in the glade, running up over his legs, taking wing, rising to the sun. The deer scratched often, and then the heat made them move again; the buck pushed under the lowest branches of a yew. In the branches above a crow rested with beak gaping, for the field cattle troughs where it drank were now below its reach.

By afternoon a dozen gulls searching the fields had found the swarming ants by chance and tumbled excitedly into the swarm. The ants became a brown cloud that rose out of the valley and above the hill. *Cak-cak!* cried the gulls falling about in the air. Some fluttered on to the grassy tracks to rest, while others at the distant coast saw the dim white movements miles away against the dark yew trees, and flew screaming to join them. At the top of the cloud were the queens and the strongest males. As others rose the queens dropped down, to shed wings and crawl back to the tunnel, their sun-life done. Through the cloud fell males, exhausted, to lie dead. Above the ants, seen as a flat smur of fog, the hobby fell an instant, struck, and the black blades of the swift that had marked summer's seconds with their beating, fell in their turn.

The deer were glad to get out of the heat of the trees and to feel the dew forming in the hill shadow. The buck grazed quickly, eager for damp grass. But the doe made him restless. The kid tried to chase his mother in play, but she did not want play with him and he wandered off on his own, watching every now and then from the meadow's edge. But she had roused him and he played his own game, of butting a curved dead bramble stem that hung like a long spiny antler at the entrance to the hideaway under the oaks. Capreol attacked the switch-horn bramble until it broke off and would not move again. He was hungry and pulled shoots of elder and sallow, but he lost interest and snatched bites of grass and thyme as he worked back to the meadow edge. When he came back in view of the other deer he stopped, for there was another deer at the far end of the meadow coming towards them. It was a heavy animal with a white flank patch of damaged hair, where a year and a winter ago it had fought off a couple of fox hounds running late and lost in the dark, hungry for warm meat. It was a switch-horn, with one long thin tine like a splint of yew branch and another curled under like a runt sheep's. Fifteen minutes before, on the hill-top, he had heard the doe call to the buck, and he had leapt from the couch of bitten bramble, for he was without a mate. One-Switch had come running along side tracks, and although there were people in the vale, not one had seen his quiet approach, for he was nothing more than a brown glimpse behind the grass. But when he came into the meadow the last bit of sun was on his one long tine like the burnish on a helmet. He came right across the meadow in a low swift run and the old buck did not see him till he was a couple of bounds away, and then he sprang round and One-Switch stopped. From among the wild parsnips the doe watched, and then she reached out and took one bite of a dog-wood shoot.

One-Switch lowered his head very slightly and started to circle the buck. The buck turned to face him on stiff legs. From the meadow edge Capreol saw the bucks' heads lowered swiftly until only their antlers could be seen, and as they charged the antlers cracked together; the sound alarmed him. He saw the old buck leap sideways, for he had felt the length of the sharp long tine upon his left temple and, knowing it to be beyond his defence if he clashed with it many more times, charged the switch-horn with a great doubling of his back legs under him and his neck arched over: and he caught the switch-horn on the ribs, on the white hair scar, which made the intruder grunt with pain and run off into the the trees. The buck chased him to the meadow end, and ran back to the doe. Capreol was alarmed at the fighting and wanted his mother. He started through the forest of plants which came above his head, but before he had gone a dozen paces a rattling of stems to his left made him stop short. It was the switch-horn, carrying its odd tine like a lance on downheld head. He had run in a fast half-circle, hoping to surprise the deer. He saw Capreol, charged him and cracked him on the withers, which made the little deer stagger into a half-fall and trip into the rough tussocks of the anthills. The sound of breaking parsnip stems made the old buck turn and come running and leaping across the meadow. One-Switch turned to meet him but saw the heavy downheld neck and ran off. He was chased right up the hill to the western trackway, and he ran down into Shannonsfield, where he thrashed and tore, and ate the buds from a garden full of roses all the night, ignoring a dog that barked itself sick to the dawn on the end of a chain.

A few days later little clouds like puffs of cannon smoke appeared. A hot wind came from the east, from the plains of Europe, the wind of a thousand miles of cornfields. That night the sky held a clear green light as the stars dipped to the north. The buck had left after the rutting to rest, and in the wood Capreol and his mother came out into a stillness that was like the bottom of the sea. There was no movement, and they seemed afraid to go far from the wood edge for everything was listening. The cloud-puffs hardly moved high up. They became black and then slowly grey-white and were hard to see. But more were coming. Only in the middle hour of night did the real darkness come. Nightjars sang again, although they were soon to leave. And in those dark hours at the turn of the night lightning lit the peaks of clouds that covered the Great Plain forty miles away.

In bed, the grey man lay with sheets thrown back, watching the faint light flickering on his bedroom ceiling, thinking of pheasant poults that would be drowned if the rain came.

The deer kept along the wood edge, feeding, but the doe would raise her head every few seconds to stare all around at strange glimmer-shapes, reverberations of light on trees that became grey and like petrified stone. Once she started at a dark shadow that moved towards them in three separate, jerky bounds, and the shadow then vanished again, for three lightning flashes of the far-off cloud had lit a bounding hare and then pitched it back into darkness. Later on a few cold rain drops splashed here and there and then there was silence again. The deer moved out into the wild parsnip meadow. The tawny owl which lived in the oak tree circled once staring down at them and flew on across the green northern sky to drink at a cattle trough in the barley field of the quails. On the nights of three weeks he had gone there; each night the water was lower and speckled with quill scurf and the bodies of blackbirds and corn buntings, which had tried to drink. Flying across the barley field the owl saw fans of light flickering from a cloud that covered the horizon.

Chapter Five

When Sirius comes back to the night sky and the white hard chip of the new moon is seen, it is the coming of autumn. This is the harvest moon, which will rise yellow on its last day; but those will be the last days of summer. It is the time of the first rains, of robins singing in the woods and pheasant cocks calling as they go up to roost in the dark. And it is the time of the stubble fires. Ribbons of flames crackle across the fields killing lady-bird and egg-carrying spider, destroying the humus of the soil. The smoke rises and carries fragments of burning straw high into the air, the smoke turns to small clouds and the charred straw drifts back to earth, many miles away. Sometimes green hedges shrivel when the flames are fanned by wind; hedge bank and field boundary with wild flowers are withered away and hedge trees are burnt under their lower boughs. The soil is scorched until the flints show like the bones of the earth, and the fields become whiter year by year.

One day at the end of August, when the harvesters roared through the nights, the old stubble fields blazed from Bey Hill to the Great Plain. Clouds began to form over the smoking fields and joined together until sudden storms swept up over the Downs.

On Strakedown the deer were lazing in their field of barley when the neighbouring field was fired. The doe smelt the smoke and was alarmed. Ancestral memory had imprinted the desire for running. But she stayed, not wanting to show herself by day. She lay in the straw with head up and ears back, listening to the crackle and the whine of pithy stems exploding three hundred yards away. Once a current rolled a wave of smoke over and into the standing barley, when she started, half rising on back legs, making the kid jump to his feet. But the smoke wave passed, and she settled. The kid browsed the dried barley leaves, not liking them but too curious to leave them alone. The sudden movement of his mother had unnerved him and he wandered round their little glade, head above the drooped ears of barley. They were rotten ripe.

A veering wind took the smell of smoke away from their field, and the kid rested his head in the barley beards and slept. Not far away, the cock quail called. It was a subdued and flattened triple note, almost a whisper, for the little cornfield bird was only twenty-six drills of standing corn from the deer. The doe heard the rustlings of its feet and the tiny cheepings of sixteen bumble-bee birds that followed close behind.

On the hill, a half mile off, the watcher heard the quails call through the crackling of the fire, and it seemed to him that it was the only living sound that would ever come again from amongst those barley fields which had sheltered so many small birds and insects through the summer. The quail called, and the sound of the fire was now the explosion of myriads of snail, ladybird, woodlouse, and young bird.

The air had gone, there was a cold sweat as of fever. Grey hanging vapours, like heat clouds, covered the hill. It was very quiet on the slope. The smoke from the fire had drifted away from the barley field, and had started up the hill, in the opposite direction. It rose straight up, turning the heat cloud above to a dark brown. The men firing the field saw that the burning was safe and were on the point of leaving.

Then one of them shouted, seeing the column of brown smoke suddenly bend above them, and a cold draught of air turned up the pale sides of the whitebeam trees on the hill behind. A wave of wind from the thunderstorms was breaking over the Downs. The wind came upon the field and threw a frieze of straw into the air. When it broke on to the lines of fire advancing slowly up the field the lines reared up and the red flames raced forward. Brown smoke tumbled into the barley field. So fierce was the force-draught into the field that the fire made its own whirlwind: the fire-lines tangled together, sucking straw and sparks into a column which roared upwards. A bending pillar of flames moved across the field and into the barley. The men ran across hot charred earth, but the fire raced ahead and was already leaving their field. They ran after the fire-devil, seeing it spreading flames across the barley field, and they stopped by the fence, watching the spout of flames and black ash rising into a ceiling of down-dimpling cloud. The thunder-storm, composed of the heat from half a thousand fires, was only five miles away.

The deer had hardly time to understand that the fire was near them before it was blocking their usual line of escape from the field. The smoke swirled at them from fires started all over the field by down-falling straw, and the doe leapt up and plunged about in the barleycorn with the kid behind her. She ran a half-circle into the middle of the forty-acre field, leaping like a springbok, feet clear of the barley ears. The whole field was ablaze. A wild roar of flame surrounded them. They turned back into a clear arena of unburned corn but they were encircled by walls of rushing brown smoke, forced up by a gale-force draught. They were trapped in a vortex from which the air was sucked, leaving a vacuum. After the sudden leaping flight they were breathing fast, but there was no air.

Tawny flames rolled into the sky like flags; sparks whirled into the brown canopy; a rain of small bright embers fell on to their coats. The doe leapt in wild zigzag, then charged the smoke wall and vanished from the arena. The kid bleated in terror, leapt like the doe, stood still, ears back, trembling like a horse struck by a bolt of lightning. The smoke blinded him, he fell on his knees, scrabbled a footing, rolled over again, lashed out with little cleaves at the binding straw. Jumped up again and ran straight into the fire. He leapt in darkness, scorched, seared; sudden bright lights beyond his closed eyes, sudden coolness again! Eyes open. A black level plain ahead, rolling and tilting, no pain, no fear, the numbness of leaping, leaping, leaping.

The men watched him go, saw his black burnt hair, watched him leap two hundred yards across the hot earth, watched him hit the three-strand wire fence around the kale field, fall back, recover, leap again at it, heard the thudder of springing wire. They turned back to the fire beating hopelessly at the edges of the flames, for it was away now towards the barley fields around the beech hanger of Strakedown. They did not see Capreol tear himself through the fence but they found the tufts of congealed burnt hair many days later, and as they tramped across the dead field they came across the blackened bodies of two small game birds shielding sixteen dead bumble-bee birds.

When he had reached the hill Capreol bleated for the doe and stumbled through the brambles and junipers of Bey Hill Down. Unable to jump anything he crawled under the brambles and yews along the pheasant tunnels and lay there exhausted, with the smell of burnt hair, bewildered by a dark roaring in his head. Hidden, Capreol lay still. When the woodcock rose and drew in the night with his dark wings, Capreol awoke again, and again bleated for his mother, and she came through the trees and licked his face, tasting the burnt hair. He rose up to her, and she licked down his flank, making it cool. (And for many days he would keep close by her, and she cleaned his scars each day until they were healed.)

In the early morning they made for the hill-top. They found a track which had been torn through bramble bines as thick as a man's finger. It led into a glade between old thorns and brambles where three heather bushes bloomed, and the woodsage and honeysuckle flowers had brought bees still draggled with dew. The grass was trampled, and a small sycamore tree had been raked by antlers and had bled sap. The master fallow, the Black Buck, had returned to the hill-top for the rut.

They lay under the shelter of a gorse bush. The sun came up out of grey faint hills and cold mists in the valleys. Spiders' webs hung limp with red dew. The old pheasant cock cockled a greeting and landed in the wet grass, his back and tail already greying with dew. Capreol lay slightly apart from the doe; he slept and the pheasant stared at him, making certain that he was not a fox lying so quietly in the dimlight, and he called his hens an alarm of sorts, one that could hardly be heard. The pheasant had lived in his thorn lands for three autumns and knew what should be there and what should not, and although he had seen them before he took no chance. The hens stood up with straight heads and necks and looked, and then vanished into the dew again, and appeared here and there like brown anthills moving. They were hunting for blackberries.

The September day burnt the dew off the leaves and the sun slid back and forth on the spiders' webs. At night the white moon of harvest rose and showed the blackened ribs where the straw had burnt on the stubble fields. The night was calm, with faint high clouds moving from the north. Capreol and the doe fed on blackberries, picking them carefully to avoid the pricks. Once Capreol pushed his nose through a spider's web and had to scrape the dewy web from his nose with a hind foot. The fire memory was leaving them but they were not yet at ease and did not much like the lumbering of the fallow deer, which came through the glade or trampled past in the wood close by in the night, as the time of their rut approached.

Chapter Six

In the dark woods of Bey Hill many bucks were assembling for the rut, and the small prickets and sorels ran excitedly over the open downs around the forest in daylight or stood watching and listening, with bellies flicking as their blood stirred. When the master buck of Bey Hill, an almost black beast, thrashed and scraped the ground in those last hot days of October's little summer, the dust rose and hung around like mist. Just before the Hunter's moon was full, a shower sent a few silver rainshot into their wallows but the soft dry dust sucked them in and they vanished. In the mornings, after the first cold nights, leaves of whitebeam dropped, pattering on to the ground like the sound of deer walking, then lay like moonbeams in the black forest. At dusk again, and every night before the moon was full, came the groaning of the bucks, a noise deep as the last tearings of wood sinew when a big tree is felled. By day the bucks rested lightly. By night young bucks came out of small thickets and old hedgerows and took up their stands in fields or by the edges of the woods. Here they would scrape and challenge the darkness and, finding it empty, move on again to any convenient stand around the edges of the big woods.

The old bucks lay in the clematis and bramble thickets surrounding groves of yew, in Kinzerlic, Marsden, Hunting Coombe, and Venus Wood: the old places, where harts had rested for centuries; the wild groves of trees, tangled and half-dying, places of woodpeckers, owls and buzzards; places where their antlers were like the tops of the old trees.

On Bey Hill the buck was nearly seven years old, a large beast with antlers spreading almost to a circle about his head: each antler alike and formed with palms nearly twice as broad as a man's hand. The Black Buck had held Bey Hill for three years. Three years before there had been a fight with the master buck, and the two had locked and pushed back and forth all night from one side of the hill summit to the other. In the morning people had seen the slots smeared in the slippery earth, each set as big as the other, for the Black Buck had been larger than any buck seen on the hill or in the valleys of the chalk downs.

In this seventh year he was a buck of the first head and his antlers were half a head taller than the others, and he would watch, and see, keeping so still, when the others would not have noticed the movements of poachers and stalkers above the bushes. The Black Buck had learnt about people when in his first year he had been stung by pellets at forty yards from a man who was shooting hares on the hill. Another year, in early summer, he had been with his does in a cornfield at evening, when the scent of man, very close, had made them turn and leap away, but there had been a double bang and one of the does had gone down on her knees in the corn as a figure ran out from behind a may bush. And the Black Buck knew of the stale scent of man along the runs and hidden ways of the hills above Storton, places where men were not usually encountered, for the scent, where it touched on a larger area of ground than usual, on twigs and branches, showed where a man had stopped and knelt, and worked for a minute or two: this meant that a fox snare had been laid, made of wire that would break a leg bone before it broke itself, and tied on to a tree root or a length of loose wood. Many times had the Black Buck heard the tinkling of the swivel links and the curdled gasps of breath in the darkness. So the Black Buck had lived on the hill, and he ran from West Holte Wood in the west to Blackbush in the east, along the ridge of Bey Hill.

So, for the third time, the old black fallow marked the edges of his territory on the hill. His country was more wild than that of most other bucks of the south country. A hundred years before it had been open sheep down, with a grove of big yews in Kinzerlic and in the valley below Blackbush. Then juniper bushes had grown between the white chalk scars of the rabbit warrens, and the slopes in those hot far-away summers had been like the hills that border the Mediterranean. Thrushes had spread the yew seed, autumn after autumn, and the tangled forest began. When the rabbits had gone and the sheep were kept in meadows in the valleys, brambles and wild clematis filled in the gaps of the yew wood and the deer trod narrow paths that no person could follow. In winter the Black Buck might be seen above Chilholte among the ash and the sycamore poles of the draughty wood near Blackbush. Many times in one year he had been seen leading fifteen does in the new plantations of

West Holte, where they had lain up under some yews near to a sheep pasture, facing the midday sun. But in autumn he made for the middle of his domain, the top of the hill, which was the wildest part of all. The grey man knew the edge of this place, but he had no knowledge of the one grassy glade of the old heath, which was an acre or more of open ground where heather grew, encircled by gorse that hid the tops of the Black Buck's antlers.

This was the summit of that hill, unknown by any man since the rabbits had gone, when the gorse and the brambles had grown up. Around this summit, hidden now in the undergrowth, were old ramparts and dykes, the defences of neolithic man. Under the grasses and heath plants were flint axes and knives, and the dull cracked lumps of flint which had been heated in the fires of three thousand years before to warm the pots of water for prehistoric man. The forest has stretched over nearly all of England, but fire and flint, and iron metal later, had turned it slowly into open down. Now the hill-top was a refuge once again, and the deer felt safe.

In the glade the grass in one corner was trodden to a dust, and the black cotyings were scattered thick. Eleven does had assembled. The Black Buck pawed the ground at evening and lumbered about the hill, working to keep his eleven does to his own, for other fallow bucks waited in the shadows for his vigilance to wane; but he kept does always round him and they slipped between the brambles without sound, peering and listening, watching the buck. And in the night the Black Buck crossed the forest track and beat the bounds of the north slopes, even among the young beech trees and pine trees in the open. Thirteen scots pines he had frayed every year, making reddish scars that half-healed with resin, but the trees never put on height and were dying. Once he tried to fray the rabbit fence, and with one jerk of his head tore a hole big enough for a roe to jump through. Part of the mesh caught on his tine and he carried it for a week until he frayed a hawthorn bush in Kinzerlic and pulled it off on the thorns.

One evening the roe came through the glade. The buck had rejoined them after resting up after the rut. They could slip under the brambles which the fallow had to leap. Capreol was curious at the scent of the old fallow buck and came into the corner of the glade near a dead yew tree which was hoary with hanging lichen. The Black Buck was lying down resting when he saw the kid coming towards him. With a grunt that belched from his throat as he struggled up, tangled in brambles, he threatened the kid, who turned in fright. Capreol ran and the Black Buck, refreshed by the encounter, trotted into the yew thickets and scraped at a patch of ground near his stand, groaning black noises at the coming night.

Capreol bounded out of the thickets in excitement. The doe dashed round in a figure of eight when they came out into the open near the tumuli. A cool wind was flowing over the hill. The buck and the kid watched her playing, almost stumbling on to her knees as she turned.

Another night they came again to feed near the hill-top mounds. It was quiet: curlew flew over against the stars. Late in the night the doe stared towards the West Holte thickets for she had heard something which disturbed her. She ran away a few yards and the others became alarmed with her. They all stood and listened. A strange sound came from along the hill towards them, with sudden slapping noises now and then like pistol cracks. From the hawthorn wood on the far side of the tumuli a long black flapping shape appeared, making across the heath. As it approached, the roe could see a head-shape familiar as that of a deer, but its pursuer terrified them and they turned and fled back down the hill, whilst the flapping monster galloped on over the brow and disappeared noisily down the north slope.

Two days later a forest worker walking back on the hill to Storton again saw the Black Buck and in the evening recounted in the 'Hare and Hounds' how the great animal had run across the hill in front of him with fifty yards of black polythene stack-sheeting trailing from his antlers 'like the devil in a bridal veil'. The man had been frightened, knowing the old stories of the haunted yew forest, but had not said so to his audience. In the morning they had gone up there, the stalker with his rifle and the grey man and twelve beaters to push out the deer from the thickets, and saw where the sheet had been torn off, round and round, from a stack at West Holte. They heard the flapping in the beech plantation on the northern slope, encircled it and chased it back and forth, but the buck disappeared near the hill-top.

Summer changed to autumn, but only by the colour of the grasses on the hill. Summer changed to autumn, but only by the hoar frost in the dells of Kinzerlic every morning. Near midday the sun brought out butterflies on the first day of November. There were new flowers of wild parsnip growing in the valley and violets on the hill. Blackberries ripened on, slowly and more slowly in the four hours of sunshine every day that was as hot as May, but still they ripened on. The birds could not eat all the berries and many ripened to the spores of mildew, sending out puffs of dust when a blackbird settled on a spine. The yew berries fell and lay and turned to purple-rusty blobs, and few were eaten, except by some of the small flock of mistle thrushes and by the deer. In the still, cool nights the boar badger came from the sett at the foot of the hill and licked up the berries, and foxes picked them up and dropped cylinders of seed, mixed with rabbit fur and mice bones, on antheaps or tussocks of grass, on the way back to the earth in the morning.

One early morning at the end of that little autumn summer a choir of song thrushes came into the forest from their crossing of the sea the day before, from Lapland. There they slipped among the dense green foliage of the yews, dropping and moving like brown leaves, sipping quiet song in that sunlight. Some thrushes sang loud again from the tops of trees when the first frosts came, but these were the birds that had bred in the vale.

It was at this time that the roe came back to the vale of Kinzerlic. The whitebeam leaves, pale as wood ash but rattling crisp under their footfalls, worried them, and they avoided them as they might a patch of open ground. Often they halted and listened. A jay gorged on acorns dropped one from half-open beak, and it rattled on to the branches and made them jump. Above them in a hollow yew the white owl which had hunted the old grassy meadows of the vale in summer stood waiting for the dusk. He no longer had to go out early, for his three young were gone from the nest in the valley tree and had flown to barns and lofts and the little church at Strake. Now he was alone, for his mate had been caught one night on a pole trap and had rattled the hanging chains when the trap tumbled till dawn, and beat it bloody with the raw sinews of her wings. All night the owl had fanned around her, calling to her to come away and landing on the stubble field beneath her, to stare with round dark eyes at the white whirling feathers swinging to and fro. The owl had gone back at dawn to hunt, so hungry were the young, until the sun drew the shadows back under the trees. When the grey man found his mate her talons closed into the fingers of his hand, for he had thought her dead. He hit her head against the post and the talons drew out eight small berries of blood as they came away. When the young had gone the owl had left the big yew tree in the valley where the nest had been. Now he waited for another night to share with the rustling bats and the mutterings of crows roosting in the yews.

When the roe passed beneath the tree again that night, already lichens of grey-blue colour like the markings in the owl's plumage were growing at the lip of the neat hole. They went on down into the valley. The breeze idled from a northern sky, thick with stars. The yew tops hummed, or were silent. Again, it was like the bottom of the sea, the old returning feelings of peace and resting. Later the breeze, thick with forming frost, moved slowly, eddying or tumbling like a tide, and stirred the night. They were stopped by a sound in the trees, a flapping noise coming only now and then. The doe led them and was the first to see a black form, lying half against a tree, bigger than a man. She came slowly nearer, ready to flee, and then the shape moved, and crackled, falling over, righting itself again. They barked in alarm and ran back some paces, but returned, finding the shape altered. Very slowly the doe crept towards it again, and there was no scent on it. As she stretched her nose to it, a yard away, it curled and crackled blackly at her, and she leapt back and stamped her feet. They encircled it in the night, fearful, but too curious to leave. There was no scent, except for the traces of a fallow buck, so they left and went on into the valley, forgetting the thing. But it was many days before the fallow deer went there again, for they had been frightened by the noise of their buck fighting off the fearful snarling, crackling enemy in the dark, the monster which had pursued him from the stack at West Holte.

At evening, still the sundogs beyond the hill, and in the last days of St Luke's little summer the watcher sat in that valley, quite still, where nothing moved save the long midday shadows, with his face and hands as brown as the oak leaves under the trees from half a year of sun. The three roe deer came into the glade and saw him, and shuffled forward, peering and touching with their muzzles all the twigs and leaves where he may have left a scent. He sat still, moving only his eyes which made them even more curious, until they came so close that if he had held out his stick he would have touched them. He saw their form, fine as a desert gazelle, more lithe than a hare, with bounding muscles drawn long by lines of tendons. Their ears were as the antennae of a moth, night guiding within the long complexities of the dark and the dangerous moments of daylight. Their muzzles, too, he saw, shining and smooth as black pebbles that live in water and know all the secrets of such close and constant touch. But their eyes – only there did he, for a second, approach the deer as an animal himself and feel their warmth, for the eyes of deer tell only movement, are not afraid like the heart and legs and ears and nose. The roe moved out of the glade and the watcher sat still for long afterwards, so that he should not disturb what he had seen.

One day, in early November, a long white cloud at great height, that stretched from horizon to horizon, moved slowly over Kinzerlic from beyond the hill to the north-west. All said it meant rain, and were glad, for the summer had gone on too long. But that night the cloud was followed by others, and they were dissolved by a little white rind of a moon, which made rainbow colours among them as if they were veils. This was the remains of the hunter's moon which had been yellow at full like the harvest moon. Now it was white; already the first winter moon. It made a new light, which gave no dimensions, and made the kid start at anthills, small bushes, and a bramble frond lying across the track. When a hare ran across their path like a little black imp, the kid leapt into the air and barked a short cough of alarm, then loped up the path with excitement, for the grass was frozen and the air smelt different and almost hurt his nostrils with its cold. In the glade near the badger sett a fallow fawn, grown big within the summer months, had felt the excitement of the first frost as well and had been enjoying herself, feeling the white rime on grasses with her lips and licking ice crystals off the bramble leaves. When the roe deer came upon her, browsing along the edge of the wood which had been her home for all of her summer life, she bucked her legs and bounded and the two young deer played, the young roe butting at the fallow's neck with a sudden surge of power in his legs. But the fallow was a young doe and did not want to butt and she leapt six times into the air with stiff legs, making the roe deer leap as well. They ran around the glade together, shaking the frost crystals off the tall dead grass stems in clouds. Boar badger setting out from the sett under the hill heard the thumping hooves and swishing of grass stems and stopped, wondering if it meant danger. He had been searching for lobworms under the trees all night but the frost had sent them below ground. Now he was very hungry and was on his way to big yews in the old grove to lap and guzzle yew berries which lay in a thick carpet under the female trees. The frosty air gripped his lungs and belly and made him incautious and then, despite his age, made him feel playful and lightheaded, and he ran his striped cheek along the white path making an icy track. He flopped on to his back and rolled until the frozen dew clung among his hairy hide; he grunted and loped on like a grey old bear. In the yews the first winter gathering of crows crouched tighter to the branches and shook black beaks deeper into frost-greying feathers on their backs. By dawn all animals and birds were glad to see the sun again.

And the next day little clouds like the feathers from a swan's breast followed the long quill of the day before. The frost faded off the hollows leaving blackened grasses and leaves, and blackbirds sipped the dew at midday. The cloud feathers drifted on over the yellow sea ten miles away, and put out the sun to the south mile by mile. In the night the rain came.

By morning the deer's coats were black with rain. On the paths the dust of summer had been washed away in a muddy stream to the dell by the pheasant wood.

Chapter Seven

In November there was a pheasant shoot in Kinzerlic. The deer, sleeping in their shelter in an island yew clump, heard the shouts and the stick-tapping half a mile away as twenty men advanced through the forest to begin the long drive of birds to the guns. The little winter sun shone on gun barrels, polished shooting sticks and red cartridges slipped into chambers, as the guns stood ready, surrounding the thickets at the lower end of the valley. Labradors and setters stood with gently waving sterns at the scent of pheasants running alarmed along the dark hillside woods turned towards them. One dog, a pointer, with bunched thigh muscles and a docked tail, whined and tugged at the lead securing it to its owner's stick, nose thrust into the gently streaming north-east wind. 'Back, sit down, damn you'; gun muzzles tapped gently on to nose, pushing the pointer back. 'Fox, I expect,' the owner informed his neighbour quietly, hoping that his dog would not break away and give chase when the beaters flushed it. A hundred yards upwind, the deer had seen the quiet encircling of their clump as a scatter of voices and sunlit fragments through the yew and privet twigs. They could scent nothing alarming, although the buck and the doe threw their muzzles into the higher air flow that now and then brought luke-warm smells of beaters and the grey man's dog. As the man spoke to the pointer they turned their heads and stared at the sounds, but they lay still. All the early summer, before they left the valley, people had walked past the clump and never knew that they were there; the deer were used to lying quiet.

From far up the valley a volley of shooting came down the wind. The guns heard the squealing of the grey man's dog, guessing that it had come upon the scent of a hare.

For five minutes the deer sat alert, becoming uneasy at the motionless figures beyond their island. More shouting from up the valley and a thuddle of wings on the air; fifteen seconds later a sun-blink in the foliage round them, a black cross hissing over, and *bang!* Before the pheasant hit the ground the buck and the doe had leapt up and were crashing out of the thicket. The kid followed after but when he broke cover they had gone, and, blinded by the sun, he ran straight at the guns. As he passed them another *bang!* that seemed to flatten all the hearing in his ears; and he leapt as he thought he never could leap, swerving as a black fluttering star crossed his sight and fell into the wood, leapt to clear anthills as high as himself, leapt over brambles that would have held him fast. The bolting deer was too much for the pointer, which sprang ten feet in its first leap of fear away from its master. Thereafter it forgot the punishment that would follow and jerked the shooting stick behind it in a race to cut off the kid before it vanished round the scattered clumps of trees. The pointer caught up with the kid at a wire fence, and lunged to pull it down by the throat. But the dog's white teeth clapped shut and jerked out of sight behind and Capreol ran a mile and a half across fields and down to West Holte while the shooting men untangled the pointer and its burden from off the wire fence.

When Capreol stopped he had run three miles, and it was three miles of unknown country across the road, down into the woods of Shannonsfield which he did not know and where there had been no deer paths for ten years; where there was wire. He had turned and crossed the road again trying to find the old ways and had lost them, for he crossed the road lower down, running into the fields of West Holte where there were no hedges, only a gentle rise to the western slopes of Bey Hill. So he turned his head to the slope, leaving black foot-holes in the chalk. He came to a belt of very thick and old yew hedge, below the hill. He slipped the wire fence, meaning to run on under cover, but after a hundred yards or so he had not the courage to leave it for the open ground again. The green hill above was like a covering cloud, the bare field that he would still have to cross to reach it was open sky; he chose to rest, feeling the nearness of the hill.

The hedge had never been cut; it was an old boundary between the farms. There were clematis binds there as thick as the deer's neck and in one place they formed a shelter beneath a yew which almost completely enclosed him. He lay and listened. The wind brought the hill down to him, and in an hour he dozed.

At night he crept out of the old hedge and started for the hill, running at first and then galloping until he plunged back into the yew trees again and was lost among the trees.

A night later he met with the buck and the doe, for she had given the whistle call which he heard along the ridge of the hill and which he remembered from the summer.

Down in the valley near to where the men had been shooting, a tawny owl sat in the branches of a hawthorn, staring at the woodland ground pattern of leaf on leaf, overlap of hawthorn, oak, or tiny twig, dead spring bud nipped a six month ago or empty snail. Other owls called but this owl did not reply or even notice. There was a movement below its perch as of a mole working beneath the ground, making a small drift of leaves rise and fall imperceptibly. The owl's eyes sharpened; it gripped and tightened on the lichen bark, wings beginning to open, but still it held. Then a small wind came and stirred the leaves, and the owl's glance moved, and the bird flew away. And all the night, while the wind came only now and then or stopped to show the stars between the twigs, the drift of dead leaves underneath the hawthorn kept moving. At daybreak the leaves formed, slowly, and became a woodcock as the grey light caught in its eye. The bird rested on its long bill, a wing dropped loose at its side. It stared at the trees around; the leaves where many times it had walked and searched for worms, and where it had courted the hen, and where it had rested beneath the holly trees, and where it had leapt up on thrumming wings to become a black star in spring and summer evenings, marking the outlines of its constellation on its roding flight. Woodcock had held dominion here, once, in summer. But summer had ended now.

Within a week of the first rains snow came that year, the first November snow for seventeen years. The wet snow, blown in off the sea at night, had lain for an hour or two, hardly covering the tufts of sheep fescue grasses in Kinzerlic. The footmarks of deer and rabbit, fox, stoat and mouse left behind in the morning, became swollen formless thaw-marks that belonged to no animals, and so the snow forgot them and they vanished.

Then in the night the warm air moved away and the stars became the night snow, and they fell for all the hours of darkness and left a great frost upon the land, and when the sun arose they gleamed and flickered still; fragments of red planets and the sapphire sparks from stars were seen on thistle stem and bramble leaf.

Another day snow came with a black north-east wind, which arose a long way beyond the Downs. As it came it froze the edges of the little spring streams all along those chalk hills where the green hart's-tongues that for ever lap the sound of rushing water became crystallized with ice. The wind roared along the gorse bushes at the top of Bey Hill and drove snow under them. At a little past midday twelve fallow deer came out of the thickets about the old encampments with coats mantled white, and trotted down into the yew forest. They were led by the Black Buck, whose antlers held frozen snow all the night like the branches of an oak.

In the grassy enclave below the badger's sett where snow, flung over the hill high above, fell down straight, deer came out, hungry, in the night and scratched the snow away to find the lichens and the green leaves of tiny herbs and orchids. A small moon came through the first thinning cloud before dawn. A hare ran across the valley, looking as big as a roe. Mice bounded, leaving clustered pinpricks for footmarks. The white owl dropped, a tiny *shrik* of fright froze in the air, and a mouse vanished in the whiteness again. The roe herded with the fallow for a time, and all their breath rose like steam of cattle. In the morning the place was trampled.

When the snow stopped late that night, it became very cold. The stars made a dull gleam like gunmetal across the valley ground. The kid liked the clear taste of the air inside his chest and he leapt about in the glade and ran a circle up to the edges of the brambles, falling over in an old rabbit hole which was covered with snow. He jumped up again and shook the snow off his coat, then galloped back, leaving a set of leaping marks: good strong leaps which showed him to be a wild deer of the hills, well-formed, able to take off from uneven ground with each foot placed securely under him. The parent roe deer watched him and caught a little of his mood, which they too had once felt for the first time. They played with him, but the old buck soon tired and stood still, listening for the other two while they butted and chased one another.

Then the doe stopped the game, for the frost was biting deep into her lungs and she felt hungry. But Capreol wanted to play and he pawed at the snow, scratching it with a front foot, suddenly leaping sideways and running again. This time he ran past the brambles and just out of sight of the two older deer. He felt hungry and started browsing yew leaves, clipping off tips here and there.

It was then that a dog fox, out looking for mice near the glade, peered through the yews, seeing only the kid. Immediately he crouched to the ground and looked about, wondering whether to approach. He had lived around Kinzerlic for three years, sometimes in an old badger sett which had fallen in and been unused for many years, sometimes in a hollow yew tree. Many times he had crossed deer trails and followed them for several hundred yards, for he had a memory. Two years before he had helped an old vixen with worn-down teeth, a berry- and beetle-crusher of the Down, drag down a young kid which had been lamed in a snare. He remembered the blood. The kid was clipping off yew leaves and Dogfox came out to the side ten feet away and ran by him.

The kid leapt around and faced the fox striking out with front legs; Dogfox stopped and crouched back on his haunches like a cat and showed all his teeth. Then the other deer ran at the fox and the thumping of hooves in the ground ran into his heart – he slipped into the yews and ran off up the hill. Long afterwards the rank smell of his water came down to them, for Dogfox had been frightened by the sudden rush of deer out of the darkness and when he was quietly by himself, towards the top of the hill, he had let his fear go back again into the ground.

In the morning the snow lay hard, and the deer moved down the valley until they came to the clumps of yew which had brambles and hawthorns growing round them. Here they lay safe, sleeping and watching: fifteen deer, unknown to anyone, despite the presence of their slot marks in the powder-snow.

Grey squirrels were leaping in the trees. They had been caught by the frost, for they had not built any dreys since the summer. They were biting yew twigs off and carrying them into the old nests for warmth. A young squirrel, born in the spring, saw the flank of a deer below him and clutched the bough, staring for several seconds before uttering a cluck of alarm. The deer lying asleep opened their eyes and the squirrel gave a hoarse squeal like a rat caught in a trap, shaking down a shower of fine snow over the deers' coats. It cried *chuck-chuck-chuck,* but the deer ignored it and it went away.

The fallow deer were restless and moved away, the sounds of their movement coming back to the three roe now and then. When all was quiet again the buck and doe slept, noses tucked into the warmth between their lower thighs. Capreol lay awake, licking the ice crystals off his fur and gazing at the strange white patterns between the bramble fronds and the little twigs below the tree. When the sun came over Strakedown the snow gleamed with brilliance beyond the tent of twigs, which made him start, remembering the gleam of sun on gun barrels and polished leather and the white bleached grasses of a month before. But the two parent deer did not move or show alarm, and he tucked nose to tail and lay there for an hour with eyes awake, watching the blue shadows outside fade and form again as the sun came and went with the clouds. At midday there were soft sounds of snow slipping off branches. A robin sang and sipped drops of water off the yew leaves. The valley was quiet all day, sheltered from the north wind, and nobody came there to see the tracks. By late afternoon, when the deer rose, they had dried out their resting places and shook dust out of their coats.

In winter, deer browse on twigs and shoots and old leaves of bramble. In a night a roebuck will fill his stomach with many pounds of food, to be slowly chewed during the day between sleeping. The kid had tried a dozen different shrubs, trees and bushes. One night, in the frost, he found a shrub he had not eaten since the summer and he tried it in hunger, for winter feeding was poor after his summer diet. It was an elder bush, growing with two others around the edges of the big yews. The kid nipped an inch off the end of a twig where a bronze bud had formed. It was strong and after two more bites he had had enough. But later in the night he remembered the taste again and returned to the bush, for the acrid leaf had bitten into his palate. This time he found something else there, which made him touch and taste with black uplifted muzzle for a minute before he took some into his mouth. These were shrivelled berries which hung inside the bush like a bunch of grapeshot. They had a peculiar, lasting flavour. He ate a few and then rose on hind legs to reach up into the bush to see what else might be there. His front legs reached out for support on the stems but missed and he started to slither down, tearing off small side shoots, and the clatter disturbed a redwing roosting above which fluttered down to the snow.

The brown owl of Kinzerlic was on a glide that was

to bring it back across the fields to the old grassland. All night it had hunted around the bale stacks and muck heaps at Welldown and had found but one mouse which it had gripped together with a claw-ful of frozen snow in its eagerness. The bones and fur of the mouse had already formed a pellet which it would cast when it stopped in the biggest yew of the valley woodland.

But the glide to the yew tree was altered: and as it crouched with puffed-out feathers the redwing was not alarmed by the thin-bowed shape that grew steadily wider in its vision. The owl's glide ended as the eight claws of its feet struck and met through bone and feather that a month before had been a thousand miles away. The young deer shied at the sudden appearance of the owl, for it flew so bold, so close, and there was ancestral fear of the talon and the short round head. But in a second the owl had gone.

The impetus of glide helped the owl on up to the old yew and the fractured branch, where it heaved and cast the mouse away and plucked the redwing's orange feathers until it reached its blood.

On that third night of frost there was movement in the air, unseen; over the ground, unheard; everywhere, of hunger frightening the hunter as well as the hunted. So the deer kept close, feeling the long hard night of winter upon them. And a grey bird came to the forests, a bird with long, taloned legs and notched beak. It fell unseen from the mists that daily covered the hill and plucked the fleeting field-fares from the yew tops. One day there was a clash of pinion on twigs above the roe, when they lay among the pines and beeches of Riallhart wood, one mile from Kinzerlic. The harrier had been chasing a blackbird and, missing its clutch at the end of the chase into the branches, turned too quickly and struck a bind of clematis at the wrist joint and was swung round, to fall into the gloom of the forest floor. It crouched on a pile of grey pine needles with beak agape, crest raised, as bits of twig and old leaves fell around it.

At morning the deer drew back under the little beech trees that stretched for a mile over old downland. They had found kale on the borders of the wood and tasted the leaves as balls of water like mercury dropped into their coats, turning their hair black by daybreak. Then they went quickly into the wood as a van came up the side of the field, and the stink of its exhaust pushed them on into the trees. At daybreak, too, the strange bird with the hooked beak and hanging legs sailed out of the beeches and flapped slowly up and down the kale field, often gliding with wings held out in the shape of a shoulder yoke. The grey man in the van did not know it for a hen harrier, slayer of chaffinches and buntings, but he watched it from the driving seat behind the mud-spotted windscreen. His gun was stuck fast between the seats by the butt heel. He whistled, throwing corn out through the door from a bucket by his legs. The harrier flew into a mud blot across his vision and for a couple of wingbeats seemed to be carrying a heavy body in its talons. It was only a couple of feet above the kale tops, beating back and forth. The grey man thought of the pheasants crouching there, noting that they were not coming to his whistle. He pulled the wheel over and steered it with his knees down an avenue between the stalks, feeling for the gun and slipping it ready round the side of the door that was held open with string.

Just then the harrier was pushing into a shallow dive. It was hungry, it had seen the dancing dots of a chaffinch flock above the green tops of the kale. It thrust almost into the leaves, then held the wings back and shook the tops of the kale in the last black line of flight. The grey man saw the whirling dots of the finches fly up before the hawk and saw, or almost saw, the dots of the pellets flying up to meet it, a slow happening in the racing of his mind which recorded also without remark the trident of a talon held to a small bird, and then the downswing of the foot before it reached the chaff-bob and the black line of one-force destroyed to become a wild parasol of feathers clawing away, a hookbeak and yellow eyes staring at his, and then a one-sided flight away back into the forest.

The deer were frightened by the shot and leapt and crushed the cracky beech branch brashings that lay all over the forest floor for a mile, until they were tired of the running and the all-oneness of the wood which they could not escape, but which became friendly again without a reason. They forgot, and thought of sleep.

Then the year went on to its small cold end. The deer came to the kale field again, because it was like part of their wood, but only when it was very dark for there had been a shoot one day, when the wet earth was smeared with nitro-powder smells, and a wounded pheasant, wing-flapping now and then on its side, in the darkness, had made them restless. They left slot-marks in the mud which froze and looked like flint arrow-heads, remaining for many days.

Another moon came and shone down the beech twigs and branches and slender boles, and was fed in a million places into the earth. For a few days pheasant cocks looked like weather vanes and were frightened at their perches and owls searched the images of blackbirds against the moon. The deer were nervous of the quietness and listened to night sounds made brittle by the frost: hares running through the woods touching twigs and brashings, sounds of cows belching a valley away near the village, mice in grass tufts, a thud when a crow died in sleep at Blackbush, oyster catchers going over in the night, piping. The moonlight froze on the grass of the rides.

Each day the sun rose red and stayed so until it vanished beyond the hill early in the afternoon. Then the hill shadow came, and the fur of hoar-crystals began to grow again. Yews under the hill went grey into the night. Woodcock dropped through the trees at Blackbush and finding the leafmould grown with veins of frost, flew on. Lapwings flew around the hills, lost in the fog. Late in the night there was movement from under the yew tree, twigs breaking and a thrumming of barbed wire. The wire snanged again. Heavy treads slipped about on the frozen earth. The ground began to ring through its crust. Two more wire sounds: *thrrringg, strunnn.* Shapes the colour of gunmetal, flat, without form, moving along the end of the field. Cracking of frozen leaves, and tearing. The Black Buck had brought his eleven does from West Holte. The fallow herd moved boldly towards the middle of the field but the roe stayed near the edge, close to the safety of the wood. The Black Buck's antlers stood high above the kale and moved this way and that as he tore at the leaves, sometimes pushing the stems down, making too much noise.

The herd moved farther still into the crop. The roe did not like this and moved off down the side of the field. Above, in some yews along the edge of the forest, pigeons sat with heads sunk into the cold kale-filled crops, squitting loose green threads of mess continually on to the ground below.

On the fifth night of moon, ponds had started to freeze in the dead forest of Anderida which had once arisen from the marshy swamps beyond the Downs, and wild duck now were flighting to the coast in pairs, with pin-tail from the alder-fringed hammer ponds. The clouds made a night rainbow that encircled the sky. The white trees, the hills white with deep frost that are the hills of night and can never be reached; the twig tips above, that fused to the moon when they passed across it, all were going. The clouds dulled, the hill was a dark line, and then that also had gone.

The deer went into the rides, they could not be seen. The wind began to roar in the yews and all the alarming sounds of the week of frost that had cracked the night had gone. They fed on fescue grass that was wet with melting ice. The wind became cold and snow came from the north-west and drove into their valley. The buck led them up the hill to Blackbush and past an old cottage with one dull yellow window in its upstairs, and a smell of woodsmoke that followed them into the thickets of the yew woods below. The doe remembered the way that she had come the summer before, a way through the brambles and under the bower-branches of yew trees, and she instinctively led that way along the hill. Then they found the hill so warm, for the storm of heavy wet flakes was falling down into the eddying air, and the yews were silent, so that they stayed, and each scratched a place to sleep. Sometime in the dawn hours they heard footsteps under the trees. Small flint pebbles and chalk pieces rolled from the steps approaching them.There was no scent, the wind going away. The buck rose and they all peered up and down. There were five deer: One-Switch, unmated, a new buck from Riallhart, his doe and their twin kids.

One-Switch had joined the family in November at the cold weather. After the rut he had lived away from the hill in a plantation somewhere near the city. He was four years old, heavy about the neck after feeding on acorns and sweet corn, and he was unafraid. Those two or three months of autumn people had seen him and marvelled at what they thought was tameness. Once a sheepdog had found him in the dusk and ran round him barking. One-Switch had charged him and caught him with the end of his lance-like tine and the dog had run off howling. But a Jack Russell terrier had been seen to play with him for several evenings, the two running round each other in the meadows. Later One-Switch had fed from a mangold clump and bitten the tops of sugar beet; he had pulled hay out of a hayrick near farm buildings. One-Switch had been seen in gardens, and people had rung the police, but he had vanished again. One-Switch had once been on the electric railway line, having somehow squirmed through the plain wire strands and he had been on the road. People had tried to approach him, and he had become a part of the beech hedge, and his tine a dogrose stem slashed off near the tip or one of the running images of the mind that move over meadows in the dusk, and then one day he had left and people wondered what it was that they had seen, on the edge of the city, and if they had seen it at all.

He kept a little apart from the others; once he had butted one of the kids and she had kept close to her mother's side. They slept under the yew trees. Later the little January sun warmed the hillside although the north wind above the hill pulled wood pigeons out of some pines and scattered them all over the sky.

Capreol lay awake feeling the transient warmth of sun from snow. There was a sidling air, the undercurrent of the wind high over them coming down the slope, but each deer had found shelter even from this. Capreol's backside was tucked into the hollow of a collapsed badger sett. The others were behind the trunks of yew trees. The doe kids were close to their mother. One-Switch lay with his back under a bramble brake a hundred yards along the hill. In the night Dogfox had smelt them all and being nearest to One-Switch had crept up to see what was there. At Christmas he had found a deer caught up in barbed wire and feasted for a week. He had come with no sound, no scent of his rankness. He had lain ten yards from One-Switch. He had waited, seeing no movement, then crept another two yards, wondering whether the deer was caught in a snare. Then he had circled, trying to press his nose closer than he dared go. At last Dogfox was three yards away, staring, sniffing, fearful, balanced for flight. One-Switch rose in a movement with neck arched up like a bow and darted at Dogfox, who leapt three feet into the air and ran into the bramble brake, tearing himself out into the night. One-Switch rested back and lay in half sleep, always watching or scenting or listening.

The cold made them hungry and the warmth from the snow-sun went just after midday. Capreol and the doe kids scented each other, muzzle to muzzle. Capreol wanted to play and butted the flank of one of them. He was stronger, with a thicker neck. Her legs were thin as ash saplings sprung up in a forest glade and just as strong. They ran up and down, trying to push one another down the slope. Capreol became so excited that he sprang up in three bounds with all four feet stiff, together. The older deer browsed on yew twigs and heather and had quantities by the time the kids had finished play. The next night One-Switch led them to feed. He was ugly in the dusk, with hanging neck and black antler marks and barb-wire scars across his back. When night came the stars wobbled in the dark for the coldest night of that winter was starting. A flock of pee-wits that had mewed at dusk settled silently on the snow. Others had gone south ahead of the snow storm. From Strakedown, a half-mile away, the deer could be seen against that snow to the watcher with his night glasses.

They came into the field. During the day, a herd of cows had been there and now their dungpats were frozen hard. The kale was splintered and broken about like the relic of a wood on old battlefields. Also, there was a strange smell which unmettled them. It was coming from among the bruised snow. It filled the whole field, hanging about in a pool, like mist. The buck went forward with muzzle casting slowly up and down to trace the smell. One-Switch had gone off by himself. He had smelt blood too many times and knew that it would not bring any good. The buck found a dark bag of blood hanging half on a kale stem. Farther on in the stems the doe found a calf, two-thirds grown, with a dull star-shine on its body like a dead salmon. She smelled it, touching it everywhere, and licked the white lips and swollen-grape eyes. She stood there with head half bent towards the dead beast tasting the smell with mouth a little open. Capreol and the doe kids were too frightened to come close but sniffed at blood spots. They left it then, but later in the night the doe came and sniffed at it again.

Another night, there being rain that froze or wet snow, and always the cold and damp, they again became very hungry and going on through the fields they came to a hedgeside where One-Switch found grains of wheat which had been thrown for the pheasants. The others came to see what he was eating. One-Switch went on ahead and found a bag of wheat in the hedge bottom, meant for the catching pens. He tried to pull a hole in the plastic, then he struck it with his hooves and ripped it open and guzzled on the wheat. He ate his fill and went on up the hedge while the others wondered whether the wheat was good to eat. One-Switch found another bag and pulled it about, smelling the wheat, although no longer hungry for it. The bag covered a pen, meant to shelter the hen pheasants caught therein. One-Switch leapt and bounded off and the other deer round. A pheasant burst up into his face from under the pen which he had pulled up with the sack. There was a wild flummer of wings as hen pheasants flew out and staggered away into the darkness, hitting the hedge trees. One-Switch leapt and bounded off and the other deer ran with him, and stopped, staring into the darkness, unsure why they were running. They gathered together from various parts of the field and trotted back to the wood, leaving the open fields to the hares, who could hide there among the flints. Again they left arrow-marks in the churned earth.

Chapter Eight

Then, one day, in their bower like a cockpit aswing above the world, the trees beginning to stream into the wind, they were as high as a buzzard soaring. The little southern hills, Trundle and Levin Down, Heyshot and Halnaker Hill, rose up around them like green clouds. They stretched and felt a coming of summer warmth. Insects, too, were rising to the benign wind, drifting up the hill slope and past them, and below, far below, tractors drew dust plumes behind them from harrowing. Down there, on Strakedown, crouched the hare, feeling the earth rising beneath him. He had found a flint, new turned and lying white with marl. He was stretched beside it, hiding. The hare's eye watched, and saw specks of rooks in ferment over Welldown copse, deer stretching on the hill, and a handful of white feathers going down the wind that was a flock of pigeons a mile away. The hare's eye watched and stared, now and then, at the flint, on his other side, at a black place where a nodule had been cracked off; an eye. It was a cavern of things in silicate, stone-frozen these many million years. But the hare's eye had yellow like the sun around the swimming of its dark fluid: so had the world improved.

The hillside showed its own dust plumes, for the wind was bursting from the crowns of yews carrying little clouds of pollen. From there Capreol could see all the field, but little that could keep his mind from wandering into sleep. Their glade was surrounded by brambles, so secure, and the porthole of fields and a little of the swaying sky did not unease them. Deer are like this in spring. But he was awake enough for any movement and he saw some of the field flints below pick up now and then and follow one another in running loops and circles. Morning sun turned the flints into dead kale stalks half standing, or hares running with bright yellow fur, or bits of barley stalk in shadow, and nearly black; whichever way it wanted. A pair of crows had landed on the field and were looking for young leverets, remembering from other years the soft heads that broke like pheasants' eggs to a tap. But the hares were running still, and the ground beneath the dust was cold, and the leverets clung to water with open arms like long drowned bodies finding life again. A hundred million years since the chalk beneath them was sinking into death; thus could the world improve.

The air was still, and the harbours coming into the land some way below the hill were the roads of the sun. The deer were content, with a warmth they had forgotten about. But one night the horse-pocks in the mud of the rides made a *cronch-cronch* sound of breaking ice when Capreol walked there, looking for water. With the return of frost the deer were thirsty. The brimstone butterfly hung back under the yew leaves, the yew flowers closed again. One-Switch went back to look for kale, but the others stayed on the hillside. In the night the wind came in from the east and brought the dark haze of the cold Arctic air. The deer went up the hill and over the top into the plantation, near Blackbush. Here there was a bank, with rabbit netting, and the wire hummed as six deer leapt it, leaving one doe kid behind. It was too high for her, and she ran up and down, slipping on the flints and loose clay. Her mother returned to her and leapt back into the wood, to encourage her over. Capreol returned and ran with her at the wire, swinging suddenly into the wood and turning back when she did not follow. Again he tried to make her jump; she was at a high place where the wire crossed a small dip, an old sheep drove. Capreol almost touched her with his muzzle and turned again into the wood. She leapt, but her back legs caught on the wire as she was going over. There she was held, balanced on her stomach, for as her front legs touched the ground and pushed back, so her back legs could just reach the sloping slippery bank behind but could give no spring-off. The wire dug into her stomach; she kicked at the ground but could only rock again. She was held by a wire strand thinner than a tendon. The doe stayed with her young one and did not feed for the whole night, but crouched there and waited.

Later, Capreol had to leave them in the plantation, for his own kind had gone on to another wood where there was shelter. They found an old place of tall trees, where the wind flayed in the upper branches. Some old trees had been felled, for their bark had been sweating with a white mould. The buck and doe found bunches of twigs like witches' brooms and juicy with beech buds. It was warm against the beech trunks, and the mossy bark was made their own colour by darkness. When they had eaten well the doe lay down, kneeling first carefully into mats of smashed twigs, then slowly lowering her hindquarters. The old buck wandered for a short time in the gloom; Capreol lay down and dozed a little, then woke and chewed on pellets of buds. They heard the old buck moving through the banks of dead leaves that had drifted into furrows by the wind. Then he settled, with only his growing antlers standing up from the leaves like two small mossy branches. The wind changed and a few snowflakes froze into their hair. Far off, up on the hill, a fox barked, making them listen. The calls moved along the hill to the plantation where they had passed through that evening. They heard the fox call again, up by Blackbush; and then it was silent.

There were hot days again, when the heat dwelt in hollows and violets came out in the turf. One afternoon the sky turned the colour of an oyster shell and the sun became a rime of pearl. In the dusk rain drove into the wood and the deer stood behind the boles of beech trees. They found straw laid out in lanes through the trees and a circle of water in an old lorry tyre cut in two, which Capreol tasted but which was dull with age. There was something else there that was curious and made him cast up and down, sniffing at everything as he slowly approached. Grey things moved in the darkness, showing and fading a little above his head. At last he got to them, and smelt rottenness.

Grey squirrels were strung by twine to twigs with fur wet-pressed with rain, as the streams of water ran over them off the beech trunks. They turned slowly on their lines as fish roll in the current of a dying sea, eyes swollen like pearls. Capreol found a crow hanging there too, that swivelled and rolled like a porpoise. The crow had come in at dusk to a roost in the witch brooms hanging on scots pines, which grew in this wood. Days before the crow had dived beneath the green waves of the yews, for safety, at the sight of the grey man. It had come into the pines near Blackbush without first circling to look for the upturned face of any man hiding there: the crow had been weary on its last flight. For three days it had dug for the drills of wheat sown in the fields of Manna Ash, that were dressed with chemicals, and it had seen the grey man too late, standing there with his back pressed to the lichens of a tree, thinking it to be a grey-green post, newly cut on its top end, showing the sapwood.

Capreol, following the doe, who did not like the pervading human taints, found the cartridge case with its sharp smell amongst the straw, and left the place. The doe looked for the buck, finding him at the wood edge. He was bending a sycamore seedling, feeling its bark and pith buds breaking off, as the stem slid through his hardening coronets. Later he nipped the last bud off from the top, having eased the itching of shedding velvet for the moment. The year was beginning again for the old deer. In the ground the buds of orchids were building cell by cell, absorbing sugars from the fungus threads of mycelium. Flowers there were, underground, a cold forming, exploring of the mould year by year, white petals, no more than scales in this March night. The doe felt her own young moving. She had heard her buck marking the sapling, knowing with her feelings what it meant; the night watched, but she fed, and it did not see her mark. The fire was coming, and the crucible of the ring, after her young had been born. The buck would know when that time was with her and would leave her alone, and she would go off again into a green harbouring. The young stirred: the buck was with her, and her grown young one would leave her. Here he fed, reaching up two yards to break off buds, antlers grown with a coronet like blind thorns soon to be stripped of velvet and burnished.

In the morning they were still there, seen only when moving as the green of the moss, as the grey of the lichens, as the brown of the leaves; whichever way the light went, they were hidden. In the dawn, before the colours, another presence was there in the wood. They did not smell or hear it. They did not see; the grey shape moved too slowly and became a shadow mixing of tree boles and branches, coming nearer: scent drifted down the hill, away. The one-time cracking of a twig was a hare running, or another deer. When the colours were there, the doe's flank was brown, shining like dry leaves.

Capreol was in the same pool of sunlight that was coming through the broken beech canopy down the hill, when the shot was fired. He did not move, seeing the doe lying down in a welter of leaves, the sun on her flank. Then he heard the buck running and barking, and still he could see nothing, waiting for the doe. There was silence. He stared into the green branches of the yew, the black spaces between the beech branches, the twig crowns, the leaf drifts, seeing white flints, chalk fragments, birds wheeling over the trees, a squirrel running. Then the doe was shaking and running in the leaves, yet she was not moving: he went to her, but her heart was spilling on the leaves, and she was going, a shadow of darkness coming over her eyes. He smelt, knowing it, knowing it was not her scent. Then he saw a movement, he leapt his own height in the air, and ran, ran, ran, into tunnels of yew, crawling on his belly into the thickets, away, away.

The doe's heart was spilling from a tiny hole in her neck, exactly where it had been planned since their slots were seen, glazed by ice, in the kale fields a half mile away at Welldown. As the grey man cut open the belly and threw out the guts he thought of the larch and beech trees that were soon to be planted on the hill and which might have been harmed by the deer, and justified the shooting, which was a few days out of season.

YEAR TWO
GAZELLE

Chapter Nine

In the third month of the year the peewits would huddle on the fields in flocks and become excited in the dusk, calling short notes and beginning their courtship, for they had noticed the lengthening days which were sometimes extended even more by a pallor in the late dusk,when the fields were snow-covered.

One night Dogfox crept down a furrow, hiding in the dark line where the sun had melted away the snow, and with ears laid flat and eyes peering like orange marbles just above the furrow lip watched a gathering of peewits ten furrows away, unable to get any closer. The birds were darting and half chasing to and fro, but suddenly they saw the top of the fox's head rising slowly above the furrow. They became a line of flints, and

Dogfox crouched, knowing his chance was going and his leap would be too late.

Capreol had found a new ground which was more than a mile east, the slope of Manna Ash Down, where the doe had wandered and followed the streams of air to Bey Hill, a year before. For many days he had hidden up in the yew bushes along the hill in a maze of small clearings that had no beginning or end, but were reached only by creeping through layered springy branches. He lay out in the grassy sunlight of late winter or in the darkness, seeming not to feel the cold or the sudden showers of sleet. His occasional bleating was heard only by the owls, hunting excitedly with the night. There had been more shots on the hill; all the scents that he knew were gone. After three days a wind came from the east and in the night he followed it to where it sprang among the hills. So one evening the little buck came out at the wood edge at Manna Ash and crossed the field corner into the valley at Hog's Common, searching for fresh grass.

For a day a cock peewit here had guarded its mate, which was crouching on a brown egg like a smooth earth clod in the barley field. It had dived fiercely at rooks, flying leisurely to a small rookery nearby, making them cry *crork* in alarm, and in its swing down from the air it had almost touched a cock pheasant which had crouched and sprung up again as if hit, to run off when the peewit flew down again.

Capreol's wanderings took him towards the hen peewit which crouched with the one egg touching each thigh-bone, and the cock saw him from across the field and fell in a slant-dive which ended in front of the deer's eyes: a sudden wild flap of white and black which made Capreol jump and run off to the wood edge. The peewit swung down again and brought a tumble of air and pinion noise over the deer's back which made his rump hairs expand into a white target, and he bucked and jumped out of the field. Then it was quiet, and the peewit rested, lying like a flat flake of flint, black markings on white, a flint new turned from clean chalk soil and broken to show the fresh black heart, a flint with a trace of marl clinging to it, where buff feathers covered the white. So the crow would see a narrow stone and pass it by and fly on, peering up and down, searching for leveret or plover's egg, loose grain, sick pigeon or diseased rabbit, a mouse running on a furrow, or the blue of a thrush's egg in a hedge.

Spring came back: by the sun that had no warmth but rose higher among boughs of the holly where Capreol lay; by the singing of the songthrush in the cherry orchard below the North Holte Woods; but by nothing else. Capreol longed for fresh grass, and buds, and wood anemones, for every bramble leaf had been scorched by the wind frosts. Often he came to the fields above Manna Ash to see if the sheltered place had brought forward any growth. Once he went another way, to the northern slope a mile away going through the valley of Windens until he came to the bare hill called Barrowdown where there was one great field stretching along the down top, the soil half cultivated and as soft as snow and with flints like crouching Arctic hares. These were the old chalk hills which over many thousand years had made a thin, rich, powder soil from the bare chalk. The wind poured like a glacier into his face and so he turned and came back into the valley of Windens, clipping yew twigs off the trees and coming to a small pine wood, which was a little sheltered.

There was an old roebuck living about this valley, with a deformed head, called Sport-head by the grey man.

Sport-head was five years old and he had been a fine animal, the antlers of six even tines, shaped well. One night, in the rut, he had chased a smaller buck over the hill and into North Holte Woods, and there he had run into a fox snare set open, without any branches to guard it from deer, drawn the noose on to his left hind foot and torn the snare off all in a stride. Then over the days the knot of wire had festered into the bone until the buck could not touch his foot to the ground. One day the foot fell off, rotten through, and the buck hobbled along the edges of the wood, feeding on dogwood and bramble leaves and grass on the rideway, and never leaving the valley of Windens again. His right antlers had grown malformed the following year, like a salt-blown beech tree where he rested in the wood, and he avoided any deer in the rut. After a while Sport-head could run slowly on his three legs, using the stump for extra speed when avoiding people in the wood.

Capreol came to where the lame buck lived and stayed with him in the same wood, never too close, but in scenting distance: the contact of one roe with another. Living thus he became more alert and watched constantly for movement. From Sport-head, Capreol learnt how to wait inside the wood edge before taking a step outside, and how to keep cover above his back in the evening light. He learnt how human scent on bushes or ground must be avoided, in case a snare was set: he learnt how the slightest human scent drifting in the evening air meant that he could never leave the wood till darkness. The lame buck had been noted by the grey man, who had him marked as a beast to be shot as soon as possible. And once in the early days a bullet had hummed past his throat and cut a small twig that fell slowly in front of his eyes. Thereafter he had hidden and come out into the night a long while after the half tame fallow, who had never forgotten their trust in man from the days of the Great Parks. So the two lived together; the one an unconscious tutor to the other, that the race might not die.

The old buck had become used to his shortened leg; it no longer hurt him. A callous had formed over the stump, and the bone was slightly flattened out. He knew his valley better than a roe usually knows a single place, for his cripple walk took him slowly and with great care. Every place he knew there.

It was mid-March, and no sign of a bluebell leaf or an orchid rosette in the woods. Every day the wind came from the north and scoured the valley, but Sport-head knew warm places. Snow fell late one night deep enough to show the dew claws as they walked, and in the morning he found a place behind old hazel stumps out in the open plantation which broke the wind and where rotted hazel leaves made a deep black tilth which was warm. There the two slept, and the young buck lay eleven yards away, having scraped out a small hollow as the old buck had done.

In woodlands the snow lies unevenly, with patches of melt and shadow and uncovered leaves where blackbirds dig and scatter, and bark where the snow cannot settle. The deer's winter coats were grey, like the bark of old hazel branches, and as they slept they were invisible. Three mornings they returned to these places, never moving against the broken white scene. But through the binoculars on the other slope they were found, after a long search, by the watcher who had seen the little buck in the autumn among the oaks of Kinzerlic. And their hiding place was marked when he returned by a tall spruce that grew nearby, before the man could distinguish the sleeping deer from grey stump roots and the black knot holes that looked like deer muzzles.

At the head of Windens, in Barrowdown Bottom Wood, was a badger sett. For those three nights while the spring snow lay unmelting in the entrance the sow curled herself round her cubs in a bed of tor-grass and moss which she had bitten and scraped off in the plantation. In the day the sun shone without heat against the air frost, while snow clung to every twig and branch of this wood. In the tunnels fifteen feet into the loamy chalk the walls were faintly lit by the midday sun, and the skin showed pink beneath the cubs' fur. Sometimes the sow snored, and nearby along another tunnel that curled round a flint bigger than her body the boar badger grunted and scraped at the cavern walls in sleep-twitching adventures of hunting and digging.

At last the frost-haze which hung like thin woodsmoke in the valley was broken up in a wind which came from the north-west. Ice-casts of twigs and bark fell to the ground and lay broken up: but frozen. The wind brought snow storms that suddenly disappeared leaving one side of the valley sky white and the other side blue. The two bucks, who had been asleep, got up as goose feathers smothered their coats and went into the wood to shelter under the brambles. Later the wind brought wet-frost, for the flakes half melted and froze again. But the wind pulled the plumes of the old douglas firs about in the valley and made the thirty-six yards of bole whip and bend, and the roots pull and heave in the earth.

In the evening Capreol felt movement everywhere as he got up out of a half-doze before daylight went. So he jumped and leapt out into the rides, leaving the cripple buck to watch at the wood edge, unaware of the ground-excitement or air-excitement which was all around them. Capreol went on another run of the woods, searching for new food, taking bites of hazel buds here and there on the hill. In the beech wood he met six fallow does who were scraping frozen snow flakes off moss, more for curiosity, for they had filled their stomachs with tattered bramble leaves since the dusk, and so were in a way content. He did not seek their company, and they hardly noticed him. So he trotted on up the ride towards the hill again, meeting round the corner Dogfox stalking a rabbit scent through the snow. Capreol stood watching while the fox came close by, nose skimming traces of foot-marks and amber stains where the rabbit had left its mark, having felt movement in the ground and the need to grip doe rabbits between its forelegs. The fox ignored the buck, for the rabbit scent was warm. It leapt sideways off the track and ran through the bushes and in a while there was a thin scream as the fox pulled the rabbit out of a shallow hole and broke its back.

The cloud-storms cleared the sky; the wind dropped. The stars came close again with frost-blink.

Capreol went back to the wild valley and found Sport-head among the hazel stumps. The old cripple looked up and blew a long breath as if in contentment.

So the weather went on, cold, with sudden violent fits of hail or snow, and a chill as had not been known to last so long. Sport-head felt the cold more, and dug deeper into the leaves for warm bedding. Once the two moved to the head of the valley where there were yew trees with branches hanging to the ground like curtains. But there was no leaf mould and only a little shelter behind the trunks.

Then there were warmer nights when the valleys were filled with rain-fog, and water runnelled for a time in grassy vehicle tracks before sinking into the chalk. The sow badger came out in the dark at six o'clock and ran hurriedly along the paths to look for worms under the beech trees down the valley. She was hungry and had to search widely for food. One night she found a mole castle up on Barrowdown and gobbled a cache of worms with bitten bodies stored by the mole in case of frost, and she ran back to the sett soon afterwards stopping to dig out a few banded snails in grass tussocks. Another night she found a litter of rabbits and crushed their milk-filled bodies one after another in a dozen movements of her jaws and afterwards felt full and ready for her young.

In a day, the sun came back again, as it does in March. A titmouse weedled with clockwork sounds all day above Capreol, collecting flakes of green lichen from an ash tree. Once it came down near his ear and caught a spider with its beak that was no bigger than a pin. It swallowed the spider, then collected its winter sheath, where the spider had hid for half a year, and carried it away and wound it among the lichen flakes to hold them together and bind them in among other lichens hanging like little ferns on branches. Later, Capreol was wakened by two ring doves wing-smacking in a pine. An old nest was there, which the doves had forgotten, slipped sideways and falling through the winter twig by twig. Capreol stretched and enjoyed the sun feeling a momentary ease. Above him field-fares chacked and chabbled, like the mountain streams they thought of a thousand miles away. When the moon was seen above the black plumes of douglas firs a woodcock crossed the sky from North Holte, a slow flapping, like a bat, squeaking and grunting, and went on a wide wood-crossing as far as Manna Ash. Capreol went out in the dusk and followed galleries up the hillside that had been burst through the brambles by the six fallow does.

It was the fourth day of April, and many of the branches of the sallow had been broken and taken away by children gathering palm. One day when the queen bumble-bees had bumbled all day among the sallow flowers on the tree which a fallow buck had nibbled in the winter, and violets had broken from the old withered turf on the tracksides, and the wild daffodils had opened in the woods; that day the mistle thrush flew to the top of the beech and settled among the crown of twigs that heaved in a grey gale of north wind. The gale, bringing snow, drove through the woods all day, breaking the palm flowers while they were yet full of honey, and the sallow tree laid them beneath its grey branches and was thin again.

When the blizzard had passed and icicles made hoary the crown of the old beech, the mistle thrush sang again to a white world, while robin and blackbird left their frozen nests. Capreol had been lying all day beneath an old yew and in early afternoon he rose, feeling hungry, and trotted through the bare beech woods, breaking the dog's mercury stems which were newly risen in the beech leaves that were crystallized with snow and ice. He came to the douglas fir plantation which rose black out of the snow. His footfalls cracked among the frozen leaves, sending a blackbird shrieking in mock terror and bringing a great tit to peer sideways at the intruder. A hare loping through the wood stopped to listen, raised itself on hindlegs, then turned and loped back, bounding suddenly in erratic leaps, looking like a small black bucking horse against the snow. Capreol arrived in the shelter of the firs as another snowstorm came into the valley, sending a cold spelter of wet flakes into the tree that stuck to the bole and froze instantly. Some of the flakes floated into the gloom of the firs like pigeon feathers. Soon the storm had brought a grey swarm of snow into the wood. The wind raged among the trees; for this was a storm bringing the fire of spring, and every creature knew it and watched, unafraid of the cold and ice. The hare crouched beneath a bramble frond and nibbled a leaf, watching with its mad yellow eyes the stems becoming crusted, then leaping up a yard into the air and skittering off with the wind, down, down, away into the wood, chasing the running eddies of wind that knocked the bluebell leaves in wild circles. In the fir bottom heavy flakes stuck in the roe's hair as the wind sucked suddenly a spout of snow into this dry place, blowing it out through the tops of the firs. The freak wind whitened the sheltered bramble beds which had remained dry through the whole of the winter snow. The sudden windgust of frost and snow startled a sheltering pigeon that had roosted with safety in the firs all winter.

When Capreol left the douglas fir grove a new moon had risen. Flakes of snow had frozen to his coat and his feet broke through a crust of snow-ice.

Chapter Ten

At this time the little buck felt an itching in his antlers that was more maddening than flies, a blood fever which made him restless and lower his head continually to low bushes and the small spruce saplings whereon he could scratch and ease the fever above his eyes. The antlers had grown to their full length for that year. They were set close together, each slightly branched in front and behind, like two halves of an old burr oak that had split and grown apart and become hoary with dead ivy clinging to it, for the antlers were grown with the velvet fur that looked coarse but was as soft as the belly fur of the wood mice which shared the plantation in the night hours. And like dead ivy the velvet was losing its hold and falling away in thin ropes, which irritated the buck as much as the flies had done in the summer.

The cripple buck had grown a stump of furred antlers like one of the old hazel coppice stools, without any form or shape. One night Sport-head caught a sapling twelve years old between his twin antlers and bent it over, stripping the gummy bark, and two days later the forester passing there along the ride saw a brown scar turning blue with hard resin.

So the grey man came that way, looking for the cripple which he remembered from the other years. The sun was almost gone behind North Holte Woods, and red squares of light looked like windows deep in the plantation reflecting back the sun. In one of these windows there was a movement. The grey man pointed his glasses and saw a roebuck scratching at the tatters on its antlers with a hindfoot. Capreol straightened and turned, and the grey man watched him move slowly across the window, one eye shining red from the sun as in night headlamps. He saw small, good antlers with brow point and top back point well formed, so he left the plantation, deciding to leave the buck after all, for the damage done to the trees was worth a good buck.

Capreol walked past the cripple who remained until the last light had gone.

For a few more days the two bucks stayed together. Sometimes Capreol lowered his antlers to Sport-head and tried to push him, sometimes he would butt his flank in play and dance round him. The cripple lowered his head too and met the young buck but did not try to push; he stood patiently waiting for the other to go away – then he would go off and scratch as best he could with his one hind leg and fray the bushes with his unformed and useless antlers.

One night Capreol wandered through the valley and out the other side into the Dean Woods, beyond the douglas firs. There were places where he had never been before and he followed the paths of fallow, badger and fox through a dense plantation of bramble and scots pine, or forced his own tracks, breaking through brambles that crossed the way, sometimes burnishing his antlers and peeling the tacky bark off the young trees, and turning in the middle of the night, after he had rested on a bed of dry pine needles, towards his own home in the valley of the cripple. But he did not go on when he was in sight of the old valley of Windens, but stayed instead in his new place, which he had marked as his own, knowing now where he was to stay.

For the first time, he was alone. He listened carefully to the night sounds, waiting for twilight before going into the rides. One day he lay out, it being a little warmer. Near his sleeping eye a spider was making its web. All the morning it worked, climbing from a grass pylon to a twig, laying the foundation. Other things were there, working. A wood ant was dragging a caterpillar, a feeble bag of parts that showed through its skin, already unresisting: the ant groped for six different footholds, legs working like galley oars, climbing grass girders that numbered a million, back to its nest. High above the spider worked, watching the sun, making ready its shining clock face of thread, ready at the time the flies would rise like spore. Above the spider a buzzard searched for rising air, casting lines back and forth across the down, that it could lay upon the sky and peering down find snake or beetle. Under the grass the beetle, on some errand of scent that came and went, followed a line to some rotting corpse of a bird, where it could lay its eggs before it died. So they watched the sun, which moving every minute made them fear that it would go too soon.

When the night came, other things began to move. Capreol heard a crying in the darkness, growing more feeble. He watched the darkness and walked fearfully round to get scent. At length there was musk rising around him and a slipping white knot tying and untying among the grass. Before him the crouched body of a rabbit was like stone as the two stoats rolled and played over it. In the night, too, without the warmth of his mother's flank next to him, he heard the scream of foxes in Windens. Owls glided by, a black movement, a drop, and a glance up, and the scritch noise of the little life of a mouse ending, enough only to make every animal nearby pause and look around. One night a fallow doe barked a deep gruff cough. It was a still night. He stopped feeding at once and ran round into the firs to circle the sound and get wind. Capreol stayed in the open ride and listened to the fallow moving about. Another doe coughed, a dry sound that could have come from anywhere in the valley below him, a valley that was too narrow to echo, a closed valley. He waited until sounds near him showed them to be coming up the hill. The does' necks rose higher against the sky. Often they stopped and looked back, ears held out like the upcurved branches of spruce. They came out of the trees and crossed near him, and a scent of men came up after them crossing in the silence and leaving him unsettled. So he went back to his hidden grove.

The woods were quiet. Often he would feed in the day. The ground was strewn with flints that shone white in the darkness or in the undersea gloom of day. Sometimes a gold and white pheasant wandered by, a bird with a tail that arched from its body like a bramble bine frosted in snow, sun, and shadow-bar. The Reeve's pheasant lived a solitary life, for it had been hatched and released in an aviary in North Holte by a man whose warmth was for birds and the colours of his woods. Many rare and ornamental pheasants were kept in the enclosure of the house at the top of the wood, but some were released, and so the Reeve's wandered wherever the woods took it, for it had no natural home. One day it came to where Capreol lay and found a few old beech mast under a line of trees, and it scrabbed the orchid tubers and pecked off the petals. At night the Reeve's flew to the top of a solitary yew tree, and in the morning it fell through the stratas of sun and leaves among the hazel and landed near Capreol again. The two kept company by their loneliness, and so Capreol stayed there in the Dean Woods. One day a wind came in among the hazel coppice woods that threw last year's leaves about and dropped them, and brought a scent of moles or woodmice now and then, or a hare in a form of ivy binds under a dead tree, or the sound of a scatter of pheasants throwing the leaves and twigs about for the old acorns. Capreol was sleeping, but the strange wind coming from many sides disturbed him, and the gold and white pheasant stood with head alert, watching through the branches, uncertain. The wood was moving in a new tide of wind. All the morning the buck was alert, except for moments when a cloud passing over dulled the shine on the ivy.

The feeling in the wind made him leap up and run suddenly along one of the paths where the fallow does ran at night. He stopped by an oak and listened. Then he thought he smelt something, for he walked back along the path with muzzle held forward. He stopped again. He was standing now in a glade of bluebells that poured scent day and night from the wood making the tops of the downs, which had been sprayed and killed of any plant, to be with scent again as they had once been a memory ago. Capreol ran again a wild circuit of the grove and then struck with his front feet at a small hazel bush, knocking away leaves and bits of bark and digging out a bluebell bulb that looked like a small soft egg. He knew not why he did this but enjoyed the pressure of the bush between his coronets and the spring back that twitched on his ear and made it sting: he attacked the bush again and broke its top with the side thrust of an antler point that was sharp as a flint edge.

Now it had become dark under the trees. Thunder tunnelled this way and that among the clouds. Then he saw a deer wading in the blackening bluebell flowers, stopping often, coming slowly along the path that he had run, muzzling the twigs and leaves and listening. She was the survivor of the roe twins who had been on the hill with them in the winter, and had fine strong legs like ash saplings.

She had been driven away by her mother at the time of the may blossoms, when the old deer had wanted to be alone again to have her young.

After the dry days of early spring and the sunlight that is cold and white like a flaring moon, when the valleys hold a sudden heat that makes the wintered grass crackle in flame, the rain comes.

For days the douglas firs hung heavy with the rain as though winter had laid its snow, and a fume of rain like smoke hung in the cavern beneath these firs, and at night the forest was alive with talk of the rain and the opening buds.

For days the stones of the valley track through Windens scraked and chabbled in a gravelly stream that carried silt and frothy bubbles and memory of a waterfall as the chalk clouded the water like milt. But the little stream lost its purpose and the glint of half-remembered fish life, and sank suddenly in a meadow a mile away where the track came on to the road.

Under the douglas firs the six fallow does ate bramble leaves and shook their coats that were black with rain. At this time they were heavy with fawns and wandered north up the douglas fir valley and lay up during the day on the dry needles among the piles of brashed fir boughs, safe from the rain. In the mornings after the rain the grass was hoary with dew and they walked back to the douglas firs with a halo of white light around their shadows.

By afternoon the rain would fall again, breaking gently on the leaves of beech and hazel like a shallow stream on pebbles. And among the cascade of spring rain hundreds of woodland birds sang until they were drenched and cold, and left the night silent to form its union with the rain sky.

In that May, a little before the time that the nightjars came back to the forest, there was a moon which arose with a bright yellow light every evening for a week. At midnight, when it rose above the standard oaks in the coppice wood, it shone on the summer coat of Capreol and the young doe so that they were a dull red, and then again their coats gleamed almost white where they reflected the light. The moon rose very low, and the valley of Windens stayed in shadow except in the last hour before the dawn when the moon had swung to the west. But in the middle of the plantation where the ancient field banks showed under bramble and norway spruce, grasshopper warblers basked in its light and sang without stopping all the night. Each in the top twigs of a large bush, they reeled an incessant song, a fall of notes like a small overspill of water drops striking thin pebbles. The two deer wandering in the galleries, cleaves shining with dew and moonlight, passed near the sounds, which then stopped. They took no notice of the songs, which were night sounds subdued within their consciousness. Other sounds like rustling bushes, the thump of human feet within the chalk bedrock or the sudden twitching squeals of hunting weasels, would override the common night sounds. But the grasshopper warbler saw a heavy shadow, a dull gleaming form, and the rattling song stopped, to start again in half a minute, hesitantly, then loud again as the yellow throat opened like a small bud.

The spruce trees of the Dean Woods had soft pale shoot buds falling from their branch tips, which were too young to support themselves. There were many flowers in the young wood, crosswort and ground ivy and clusters of white flowers on the wayfaring tree like the small flat clouds forming from the warm day-air still rising from valleys across the downs. The feeding was very good, and the deer wandered slowly along, taking a beech leaf or flower of cocksfoot grass at every step, without even having to lower their heads.

In the dusk the badger cubs came to the sett entrance in the wood in Barrowdown Bottom, waiting behind the sow like little striped ferrets. She touched every scent with her black wet snout and sometimes moved forward a little the better to catch a smell which puzzled her. Smells of dead mouse, pheasant droppings, growing grass, the leaf mould of the wood; the deer. All had to be tried before she let the cubs out to run about and crash through the grass jungle. Then they would rout along mouse trails snorting through the grass with snout-snufflings and excited wheezing. They found black slugs making glistening tracks of the moonlight, and they caught large beetles that were endlessly climbing the dew-drooping grass stems. Later in the night the cubs returned into the sett to doze, but in twenty minutes they came out again and roistered in the long grass. One cub found a tiny mouse hole in the trackway with an exciting smell twining the night like an invisible honeysuckle bind. The cub followed down the scent stem and started to dig, nipping at pieces of grass root, thrusting small black nose into the cavern it made and snorting, coming finally to a small mossy nest which shook with a startling vibrating whine. The cub touched the moss and jumped back as it started to move again. Then another cub came across to look and the first cub snapsnarled at its ear and pulled the moss bundle to pieces with claws and mouth, the while pushing its brother out of the way with its flank. Soon it had discovered the origin of the sweet smell, for it found a little brown wax pot filled with honey and pollen and five cells with white bumble-bee grub inside. The queen bumble-bee, which had laboured for four weeks at many hundreds of flowers to start her family, was champed between the cub's flat grinding molar teeth.

Soon the nightjars came back, and it was the time of skies lightened long into the night by the first days of summer, come at last to the cold northern hemisphere. For all of May the evenings were still, with purple vapour bands beyond North Holte Woods.

Sometimes there were sundogs as the sun was setting: two pale rainbows in the sky fine-tempered by the northern winds. There was no rain all the month, except for one day when a thunderstorm set the gravel tracks chattering with washing stones.

Chapter Eleven

It was summer again, and there was a fever for the renewal of life before summer should end. So the nightjars drummed the air by night and the woodpeckers drummed the trees by day, and wood warblers sang in the beech groves again, and a woodlark rose high over the douglas firs, dropping its song down into the wood. Always the buck and the doe were together in the Dean Woods.

At dusk the nightjars awoke and flew the wood edges silently like sharpwinged owls, hovering with fast-beating wings in their search for the ghost-swift moths which swayed above the grasses. Their little whiteness was covered by the larger shadow and so snuffed out.

One night the deer came near to a nightjar's two downy young, which gaped like frogs and crouched side-by-side on a patch of bare ground beneath overhanging brambles. The hen bird, which had left her nest to gather moths when the dew had begun to mantle her burnt-bracken feathers, saw the roe moving about near to her chicks and flew quickly over, clapping wings in alarm. The roe walked on: the nightjar cried *quoit-quoit-quoit* and flew at the roes' legs, flicking upwards in their faces and gliding round them with wings held high above its body. The doe stopped and nodded in play at this strange bird, lifting a front leg rather stiffly as if to strike it.

The nightjar landed on a spruce tip that was half uncurling with new growth, and scarcely bent it: lay there, drooped like a swift, losing as it touched the earth all its nightly form, and became a ghost of day. But when it rose again the nightjar played with night, flying on the edge of darkness, seen a moment, vanishing again, the white tips of wings and tail like pale moths.

And the cock nightjar, every dusk, perched high among the douglas firs, opened its frog mouth and jarred the first stars, a call of cicadas and night frogs, a greater silence and a greater darkness, that the fading purple of this night only dreamed about.

Below the nightjar: sounds of bracken, bramble, and the tall woodland grasses being crushed and pulled, the six fallow does moving. A sea-fog came in the darkness, curds of formless cloud that shrouded Bey Hill and glowed in the orange light of the far lights of the city. A moon two days waning rose over the hill and the sea-fog swung the beams through gaps like a lightship. The sea siren beyond Selse boomed a dead note; three times the note, then silence: three times again. The fog came into the forest, no wind with it, the firs stood like steeples, the fog creeping in. Scent of honeysuckle dried up by day now unfurled and spread in tendrils through the trees, the moths moving among the blossoms: dog-roses and tall umbellifer, flowers of hedge bedstraw and campion, white and staring in the dark.

By morning the scum of fog had turned white in all the valleys long before men were about, and the tops of the downs were made islands.

So they passed their second summer, a summer of flowers.

One day a fast fly that whirred out of the sky settled on Capreol's flank. Its wings were a gauze of green and red, which the sun radiated now and then as the fly turned this and that way among the buck's coat. It was looking for an opening in the buck's hair. Its face was black, as was its body, with a thin needle like a blackthorn spine for a mouth. Capreol was sleeping. Gently the fly reached forward among the hairs and thrust down its tongue and cut a hole into his skin. At once he awoke and shook it away. It looped a black twine of flight over his head, and settled back on the deer's flank. Capreol shook it away. The fly settled on a leaf. But the smell was too great, for it had not sucked blood for a day, and it wanted to feed the eggs forming in its body, and in a while it came back. The buck was dozing but woke before the warble fly settled on his ribs. He jumped up and, followed by the doe, was off through the bushes, stopping to listen now and then for the drone, a fear of sound bred into them. For a while they found a little peace under a hazel stump, sheltered from the sun. But the fly came again, and they moved on.

And so it was, when each day had gone and night began to rise first from the deep hollows of the spruce groves in Windens, that the roe would leave their warm bed and wander into their plantation, breaking the damp embrace of night and day.

Soon the days were too hot for them, so one morning they walked north out of the wood and over the down crest where barley dipped them in dew up to their shoulders and they couched on the far slope of the down where it was north-facing. Below, mile upon mile away was the land of the Weald, blue to the hills of Surrey, old Anderida, where great deer once roamed and the wolf had run.

The raspberry thickets hid them and they slept. In the noon, when the sun moved round, Capreol woke and bit off a few raspberry shoots, some with berries on them; but his eyes closed again before he had finished and a red fruit hung at his lip until he woke again.

This time a movement caught his eye. Something was creeping like a small mouse on a dead thistle stalk just in front of him. He stared with curiosity. A large moth with a black and white furry stripe running from head to wing tip, like the colours of a badger's mask, was shuffling around to change position on its resting place. It faced head upwards and slept again. Two days before it had hatched from its brown torpedoe chrysalis under a bramble bush, and its night with the moon and the bell bine flowers which blew white notes in the dark had made it tired. When it had settled again, clasping, it became invisible, a convolvulus hawk-moth grown to a thistle stem.

Capreol dozed again after the moth had passed from his mind, but awoke often. In the afternoon, when the sun came to see the northern hill slope, warm air formed of the scents from hayfields rose off the lowland plain and came close by in a ferment of little clouds, that faded again when they had gone beyond the hill. Once a whitethroat warbler sat six feet away and made alarm notes, clutching meanwhile in its beak three small caterpillars. Several times in the morning it had tried to frighten the intruders away while its young perched in their goose-grass cradle on the other side of the thicket, but the deer had not heard it.

Then a pair of dunnocks crept through the canes calling, daring to sit and stare at the animal in their territory. Other birds there were, with nests and young. Every three minutes a meadow pipit, after great effort, wound itself into the sky with a sound like a small ratchet, to drop again fifty feet to the ground on wings held out like parachutes.

When whitethroat and dunnock and the stippled meadow pipit were wing-tucked from the dew, and the convolvulus moth might have been a night hawk high up, so fast it flew, then the deer rose, ready for the night.

Now the little buck found the fever mounting in his blood. In the denes or wooded valleys, his territory, he wandered and beat with his antlers small bushes or twigs overlaying the rides and clearings, scraping with his forefeet and leaving a mark, and twig-cuts and wilted leaves, and a scent from his hock glands. Then, when he had marked the young beech woods as far as the daffodil copse, he found a young plantation of dense cover, and good feeding, and there stayed.

In the morning, in the glades and beneath the beeches the sun moved many hot pools of light among the black beech leaves making a shadow-mixing of movement in a spring breeze, hiding the six fallow does whose backs were a forest floor in sun a-move. To one side of his ground, down there in the douglas fir valley, it was beneath the sea where light did not enter, and squirrels or mice or moving deer were grey, with only a sometimes look of the earth. He heard blackbird's song, and the chaffinch, and the calls of golden-crested wrens high up in the larch trees like fir cones ice-covered and ringing in a small wind. But he was wild, and he did not notice them, for only if the notes changed to an alarm did they come into his consciousness.

Summer made the leaves dusty with a dull, fading green. Capreol had become a movement over the forest floor as regular as the daily movement of shadows, as he visited the boundaries of his territory with the doe always near him. Often he stood still, listening for sounds of any other buck that might be prowling, sometimes chasing twigs moving gently in breeze and beating them with his antlers.

Once an owl dropped in the gloom before songlight, ending the wanderings of a rat. It crouched over the body near the buck, whilst its three young screeched for food from a branch four feet above them, climbing down through the leaves and dropping one by one to the ground. They flapped grey downy-quill wings at the old bird and cried with open hook beaks into its face as it tore the rat to pieces. The flapping and skirling made the buck charge them all with lowered head, catching one young bird in his antlers where, in terror, it pinned an ear with four claws. The old bird dashed at the buck, hitting him with open claws across the neck. Capreol sprang round to meet this attack but found the bird had gone. It dived again, he leapt about to face it from another direction, with the owlet staring with round eyes and gaping beak, locked by its talons and unable to release itself from fear. The buck ran round in a wild canter shaking his head, then stood still, not knowing what to face, which gave the young bird a chance to flap away into the trees.

In the days after midsummer Capreol followed his doe and often chased her as she ran a twisting knot of paths and ring-runs around the trees. Then one evening there was a scent of another buck. Capreol followed the scent upwind through hazel clumps, past the old beech and the orchid glade, on beyond the wild daffodil glades, and nearly to the douglas fir valley. There he listened, hearing twigs cracking, and then caught the smell very close of the buck that came at a gallop without any warning from under the oaks and hazel.

Capreol turned, and One-Switch stopped one leap distant. For the time that it took a squirrel to jump into a tree and run to the crown, they looked at one another. This buck had one long tine, like a unicorn, and the other tine was curled back like an Arab-knife. Before Capreol could run away One-Switch leapt at the smaller deer with the strength of both his back legs. Capreol was late in meeting the thrust and the long tine caught between his antlers and pulled his head sideways and he was on his knees in the oak mould. But the switch-horn's tine slipped the lock and when he had faced about again Capreol was up, ready. They leapt into each other, meeting fairly, coronet to coronet. Now One-Switch pushed and Capreol held, but the weight was on him and he was on the down slope. He went back, held for a second in a root with his two back feet, then lost this hold and the back legs were sliding on soft mud, the damp earth under the mould. He dug cleaves into the mud, the muscles locked but One-Switch pushed him and he could not hold. The mud squeezed from between his cleaves, and One-Switch pushed him into a tree where he held fast. Now Capreol buckled his legs beneath him, braced into the tree, and strained and levered. For a minute they held necks bowed, points locked, and their breath went up like steam. Then the tendons began to shake in the switch's leg; he was blacker than the Bey Hill buck in the shadow, and he was old, and he knew he must break the strange weight of the young buck. He braced, then snatched back his head; Capreol fell forward, One-Switch struck again on the rebound under the throat, and the point scored down the wind-pipe into Capreol's chest and sank in. The small deer shook himself away and ran off, but galloped back looking for the doe who came to him. One-Switch was ready for this and cut her off, butting her in the ribs, then chasing the little buck through the brambles.

Once Capreol fell, caught by a bramble bind around his legs and One-Switch rattled his point across his ribs. When he had gone One-Switch returned to the young doe and they stood watching the night, the noises of hares running on the leaves all around, the calls of owls and nightjars in the plantation. They listened and waited as the moon went on and the doe put her head down and found the cooling scent in the splayed and sliding marks on the tree and on the tine of the switch-horn.

Capreol ran far enough from One-Switch to be sure that he was not being chased any more. Then he stopped and listened for a long while, hearing the scampering of mice and rabbits here and there, waiting for the familiar sounds of deer feet quietly pounding the grass and rootlets of the forest floor. He moved on, sliding in and out of shadow, stopping, watching the night, hearing everything minutely, fearing. The wound in his throat began to throb and he tried to lick at it. Later he went down into the dell; moving around the territory he caught a little wave of scent from the doe in the higher air. He stood on hind legs, resting front feet against hazel wands, but the scent passed. He did not feed at all, but he lay down when the moon went in the last hours of the night and the wood turned black. He slept a little. But before the nightjar had stopped singing he was up again, searching for any signs of the doe that might come on the wind. The wound made him limp on the left foreleg, but he came up through the wood again for fifty yards to listen near the top of the valley slope. There was no sound. He went on, feeling his way by scent, touching the bark and tree stems of the coppice, the crushed daffodil leaves where he had fled away into the dell, the scent of the rabbits and hares that had passed and returned, a pellet of mouse fur cast by an owl. Then he came to the scent of the switch, and he drew back a step and stared again. Memory of the doe made him go on and he came to the scene of their fighting, and his rump hair stood out as he came back into the arena of the stand. The switch scent was thick on the leaves, the small twigs, the coppice shoots and in the oak mould, everywhere. There was the scent of blood and the scent of the doe which he smelt closely. But there was no sound in the wood until the blackbirds began to sing, and he went away, back down the dell between the fir boles.

For a day he rested. The Reeve's pheasant found him and Capreol slept secure while the bird gave no alarm. But he woke when the pheasant began to strut before the roost. All at once Capreol leapt up and charged, making the pheasant blaze a trail into the trees. He jumped about and skinned the peel on another hazel stem. He shook his head and pawed a red patch of sunlight. He ran through the firs and listened, standing to the darkness. A shrew ran over his foot. There was nothing in the wood. He lay down on a rideway in an open place, but did not sleep or rest. The forest was becoming old with night.

For a week he ran among the trees, making a web of his own among the places where One-Switch was running with the young doe. He slept by midday, seen by many, on any bed of leaves where he might be standing when the August sun made the wood stop with heat. In his own darkness of sleep the eye of One-Switch drove him to his knees, and the point had the shine of the sun upon it. Sometimes he watched them through the leaves and twigs and once dared to come into the glade, but One-Switch chased him away.

After a few days the fever of the rut had gone. Somewhere behind the forest trees, in glades or on grassy earthworks where the trees would never grow, the natural clearings, the roe bucks of the forest had run their does and were now hidden, unseen by most people who walked the woods. Far down in the woods too were the does, quiet again, feeding at first light or in the night, going among the thistle stalks, watching. In them was the buck's seed, unmated with the womb until the time of the frosts.

One day the watcher walked past Capreol as he lay asleep; the man stopped and looked with wonder at the finest antlers he had ever seen on so young a roebuck, brow and top back point of even length, polished hard like two yew branches rubbed together for a year in a clacking wind top tree. How well and even-shaped they were. The man walked on quietly and made a note in a book when he was up the hill, thinking how, in a year or two, this would be a buck of 'great renown'.

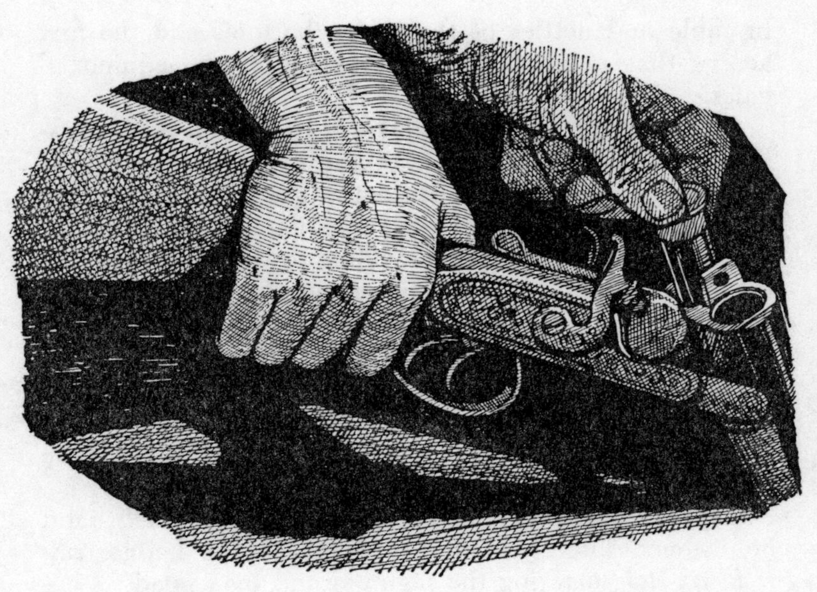

Chapter Twelve

Capreol moved only by night. By day he was a brown hazel stump, or a furrow of beech leaves in the sun of quiet September mornings, or a brown beech faggot left lying in a dark corner. By night he became a grass tuft rank-grown round old cow dungs, or a straw bale soddened by rains, or the first gloom of night at a ride end. He could stay as still as any dead tree, or he could float in a meadow middle until, watching from the wood edge, the grey man saw shapes chasing in a score of places, and all that vanished. Places he had that no one ever thought to look for a deer, and he would travel far, keeping in the sheltered places wherever the wind might be. Sometimes he ran into the fields and followed the hedge for miles, finding little crab apples lying in the bramble and nettles of the hedge bottoms and the first acorns that were shaken off green after the equinoxial gales.

One night he followed the track to Manna Ash, crossing the road of flint cores fractured by ironbound wheels a hundred years before. Here the grey man's dogs ran twice daily; the hairs of his rump flared with warning, and he waited at the gate unwilling to walk farther along the lane with its rank canine smells. In the bottoms of the woods owls cried, and the stars of Orion began to rise. It was an hour past midnight. The moon cleared cloud; it was low yet had a strange whiteness, for winter was coming. Shadows of branches on the road looked like the blackened bones emerging from a deer corpse quick-rotted in the summer heat.

Capreol was made anxious by the dog smells, and he listened intently. Crickets called in the hedge, *riz-rick, riz-rick,* marking the night second by second.

Far down the lane a hare loped off the meadow, wet with dew, to return home to Windens along the dry lane. Capreol heard the scattering of gravel specks off its paws, and waited. In a moment the hare appeared and Capreol, made alert by the smell of cold air and dog scent, stamped a hoof into the gravel. The bobbing hindquarters sank, the hare rose to watch like a black and white striped demon, ten yards away. For a moment the two stared at one another. The hare was unable to separate the deer from hawthorn shadows behind, but then it saw a watching form and got a whiff of old scent from the grey man's evening walk, and it bolted through the hedge. Capreol leapt, startled, through a gate, and trotted along a field bank to Windens another way, barking twice, without stopping, exhilarated by the encounter.

Here he met another night wanderer who grunted and champed and tore out earth clods and stones from a bank. But Capreol was not alarmed, for the night was of cold dew and grass and the hoary smell was of a badger working.

It was the old boar who had been in the chalk cavern in Barrowdown Bottom the last winter through. He was excited, for he had found a big wasps' nest, and he only glanced at Capreol having smelt him a long way since. Wasps almost overcome by cold crawled in a dozen places through his hair, unable to hook their stings into the skin. The badger had a net of roots to move before the nest; with his mouth he pulled out a flint like a mammoth tooth embedded in the roots a hundred years before and slung it to one side. Soon he had a hole big enough for his snout and he snorted through the roots, smelling the larvae. In another ten seconds his teeth had sliced a root thicker than a man's finger, and with closed eyes he thrust his head into the roaring chamber, gulping the sleeping white wasp grubs in their paper beds. When he had done, the boar sat down and scratched his hide with such a thumping that rabbits went running for their buries a hundred yards off, and Capreol, now nearly a quarter mile off in the woodland where he had sheltered with the cripple buck, stood listening. Capreol had come back to hunt for companionship after the disappointments of the rut, remembering the sanctuary of Windens and the cripple buck.

He walked through the trees and the maze of hazel coppice stumps, remembering the ways. Now and then the companionship of old Sport-head came to him, and he sniffed the leaves, trees, path: anywhere that a scent might be. He went into the coombe bottom and looked under the old yews where they had searched for warmth. He searched by the badger sett where they had lain when the white rime and a snow-frost had made tiny wind-bells of the larch twigs. For a long while he stood in the pine wood, with the mask of wood shadows about him on the ground, the pattern like deer bones that moved ever so gently in time with the moving night, leaving behind, as the moon went on, one tiny place beneath the pines, where the patterns did not move, and never would, again.

The sun was low slanting in autumn, warm where a bank caught the last light of summer. The sun reflected from all the leaves from Windens to Bey Hill: there was a shine on the land. Capreol lay in the warmth and dozed.

He had found a bed of moss under a beech tree that was a strange shape. The tree had been left on one of the slopes that faced the glitter of the English sea ten miles away: it had been left because, one of the foresters said, it was so crabbed that to knock it over would bring bad luck. The tree had grown on a patch of pure chalk thrown out of a badger warren two centuries before, and while the other beeches of that place had grown in unity, tall and straight, the old beech had through a series of mishaps been left open to the sea wind, and had been shrunken by the salt-blast. Its trunk had grown parallel with the ground, for the salt wind had funnelled through a gap in the woods, scorching every bud that dared to open on to the west. Each year the tree had guarded a few buds from the wind with its ageing trunk sprouting tufts of twigs and bulbous growths that cracked and swelled again with disease, but holding always those buds away from the wind. Now the plantation had enclosed it, and four small green leaves had opened to windward, for the first time. Many nights he spent beneath this trunk, feeling safe. But now there was something wrong with the wood.

Two days before it had been sprayed to kill all broad-leaved trees. The scent of the spray had been washed away by the rain, yet it still clung as minute hardened beads to the webs of the orb-web spider. The female spiders moved sluggishly over their webs, feeling the trap-dens of the dogwood leaves pulled together by silk, where they slept by night. But the leaves were hard, shrivelled not to the dark wine colours of autumn but to the grey ashy colours as when leaves are scorched by fire. There was no shine within this valley, only the stripes of green and grey: the lines of spruce and the dead shrubs down into the valley and up the far side to the yew clumps of Barrowdown. Many of the chalk flowers were shrivelled by the spray along the tracks and the earthwork banks where Stone Age man had made his fields: violet petals of felwort, wrinkled up and turned the colour of dead skin, the pink flowers of common centaury, the last frog orchids and the autumn hawkbit.

Capreol liked the sunny banks, and he dozed all the days of the last sun around the time of the harvest moon. But at night the smell of the spray came back, the blighted leaves bled back their scent into the dew night, and the caterpillars, the spiders that died and rotted by day, turned the night air musky. The buck left Windens that night and went to the hazel thickets in the Dean Woods behind Manna Ash, the territory he had held at the rut. He wandered down the rides trimmed back by the grey man, and was frightened by a black shape at the end of the ride. In the instant he thought that it was a man and he fell over in fright, ran on a few paces and stamped the ground with backing leaps, and barked. He ran off up the ride, then stopped and looked back. A pheasant called with alarm. The spectre did not move. He stood silently and watched. Then he became curious and moved forward. The moonlight patterns slid along his back as though he were a smooth boulder under waterflow. He circled the shape, cracking a twig or two under the hazels. The pheasant which had called peered down, snug against an oak trunk. The moonlight made it restless, which the excitement of a spring day and the first new light of the year will bring. It was ready to shout again into the still night and make its voice echo against the blue-black line of Bey Hill.

Capreol moved around until he found the faded scent of dog and man, the same scent which faintly encumbered the woods most nights, harmless as long as they were cold. But there were other scents which aroused his curiosity more, and the buck approached slowly until, with neck outstretched, he touched the frightening black shape, muzzling lightly and recoiling, touching and tasting the multitude of strange scents – rats, tractor oil, oiled twine, cartshed dust and tobacco smoke which had been brought up on a pile of straw bales stood for the pheasants to scratch beneath.

Beyond the straw bales was the edge of the wood, and a meadow stretching across to other outliers of the same wood, a beech hanger, and below, in the valley of Manna Ash, a fir copse. Capreol liked the scent of the grass and ducking his head beneath the middle wire curled up front feet and sprang through, leaving a tuft of foxy hair on a barb. Rabbits feeding in the pasture bolted at the sound of the wire springing on the posts and crouched in the moon-shadows of trees, the same safe shadow-islands whereon sometimes they hid by day when the meadow was a hot dangerous sea of sunlight.

The meadow had that morning held cows, the warmth of their breath and the smell of fresh dung-pats rose as a pleasant fume into the night. Large beetles droned about, seeking the cowpats wherein to lay their eggs.

A fox was on the meadow. On these nights a fox could travel easily into the places where rabbits were out feeding, by slipping quietly from shadow to shadow and running out on a rabbit before it could get to the wood. The fox had been cutting one corner of the meadow to get behind the rabbits; now the buck had spoilt its stalk and it trotted on down the edge of the wood towards the fir copse, paying no attention to the moon-grey forms that jerked back into the wood in front of it as if pulled suddenly on strings. No rabbit was worth a chase in undergrowth where it bounced around tree boles and thicket like a billiard ball, back into its burrow. So while Capreol grazed the strangely fresh and dewy grass, the fox scented along the wire fence and on towards the fir copse near to a pair of cottages.

But before it had started its stalk on the rabbits which lived there it caught a stronger scent of chickens which had just been brought in coops in the garden of one of the cottages. Slipping the garden fence it slunk up to a coop wherein six pullets dozed. The pullets saw it but the rank stink of the fox as it circled the coop made them huddle silent and alarmed. Then the fox, finding no entry, started to dig. The pullets cackled and fluttered, and the fox tore at the bars of the coop as it would rip tree roots when digging an earth. A window pane in the cottage, reflecting a warped and full little moon in its dirty glass, moved open, and the moon image flew up and vanished. The buck saw the movement and barked. The fox heard the warning amid the commotion and slid away from the coop. There was an orange stab of flame and a bang: the fox became another moon shadow, crushed by a hundred pellets as large as grapepips. The buck turned and ran up the meadow as another bang came from the cottage and buckshot balled in the hair along his spine and stung his hams. He grunted once in pain, then did not bark again, but flew up the meadow to the trees, almost crashing the wire fence but turning in time and clearing it with a leap that took him six feet into the air. On the other side he somersaulted twice, jumped up, fell again as back legs overran front. He tumbled into a drift of beech leaves along the track that he picked up, leading through a stand of old beech.

Capreol ran a mile to an old douglas fir grove, which was as dark as the yew grove. When he stopped, mist rose in one narrow moonbeam from his breath. But the shock of the pain was still with him and he suddenly started forward again, running haphazardly for a hundred yards before stopping again and trotting or walking on. There were five fallows under the firs, a herd of does with one buck on a rutting stand. But Capreol did not seek their company. He had found one of their galleries and it led out of the wood to a valley of oaks, stagheaded by age and the chalky land, the southern edge of the Dean Woods and just over a mile from East Holte, in a place called the Warren.

He wandered the crossing paths all night, occasionally stopping to browse a few leaves of dogwood, thorn or hazel. Twice he smelt the scent of other roe, a buck and two does, but it was old scent of the night before, and he followed it but a little way before cringing with the thought of pain and leaping off at another angle. Sometimes he stopped and stared back the way he had come for several minutes. He remembered the deadly multiplication of lights which had come before his pain; the flashing moon; the steely gleam; the orange flame. But the only lights in this dark place were two dull orange glows, one to the north and one to west, the far-off lights of cities showing in the sky.

By dawn Capreol had gone more than eight miles, but he had doubled his tracks through unknown paths and was still in the Warren Woods. Once he had been on the ridge of the downs where the land slipped away to the Weald and a constellation of moving lights of cars far below. At dawn he was in a plantation, a place of tall young scots pine, and he found a bed of grey pine needles, like the hill plantation where he had lain up with his mother the year before on Bey Hill. His back legs ached with the bruisings of the shot, and along his spine pellets had raked raw lines. These he licked, eyes closed, for over an hour. A robin sang, perched on a dry bramble stem a yard above the buck. Once a jay hopped down through the pine twigs, peering and muttering to itself. The year before it had pecked out the eyes of a dead fallow which had been wounded at a drive, when the buckshot had scored half a dozen sides of deer. But the buck, which had been dozing for a few seconds, awoke and ran his tongue again across his back, and the jay flew to the oak woods down the hill to look for acorns. Mice ran across the pine needles and in the twigs above the ground a hedge sparrow crept. There was nothing else.

The scores across his back, so close to the spinal cord, healed easily, leaving white marks that ran diagonally in the hair and marked him for the rest of his life. The pellets in the back legs caused a lameness for several days, then became embedded in callouses in the flesh.

Capreol did not leave the Warren for many weeks. It was milder even than Windens, being enclosed by older trees, and the sky was hidden by a canopy of oak leaves. Occasionally at evening there was a smell of diesel fumes as the grey man's van passed two hundred yards away; by day the far-off whining of chain-saws in the older woods below: by night the wild raspberry thickets and the silence, silence of the greatest woods of southern England.

Chapter Thirteen

In October, before the forest had quickened into autumn, the fallow does and bucks assembled in the yew groves and the old thorn thickets in the valleys. It was the time of the rut. The does came in small herds to these trysting places, running the forest paths by night, nibbling white scars on the branches and trunks of saplings of ash or sallow: marks known by the bucks who followed. The deer came from many woods and groves. They ran the woods by day as well as by night, and the cleaves were found pressed into the mud in many a ride and path where they had not been seen during the year. The mud slots pointed like arrows to the valleys and coombes folded deep among the downs – Kinzerlic, Marden, Harting Coombe, and Venus Wood. In that year a sorel fallow buck was the first to be heard groaning, at the end of summer, as the mistle thrushes clacked in the yew trees among the berries. The sorel thrashed stems of kale on the edge of a field at Storton while a fallow doe watched. The doe stayed with the sorel for a few days but left when three more does came into the forest and the Black Buck began to groan. A week later the sorel was chased from Storton and ran to Hacksway leaping the fence of the main road and nearly running into a car. Blinded by the headlights, he stumbled against the second fence, grazing his flank on the barbed wire. He kept to the road then, and trotted down the hill that led to the valley of Hacksway to Clorys Down. As his cleaves rasped dryly on the road, near the door of a public house, a black mongrel barked and was booted out to investigate the night sounds. It chased the buck a dozen yards up the track into the wood before returning to water the paling fence of the inn's garden and disentangle the intricacies of scents on car wheels in the pub yard. It watered half a score of tyres before returning to the massive hearth and embers of the stone-walled cottage pub. Deer were no longer of interest to the dog; often they wandered by this place in the woods. The landlord had heard the groans of buck for fifty years in Clorys Wood. The sorel ran on, along the Downs, to Barrowdown, and took refuge in Windens.

The first rains of autumn put out the summer warmth on the Downs, and the yew woods of Bey Hill were black as drenched embers and steamed day after day. Under the yews, near the devil's humps on the spine of the hill, the Black Buck paraded in the gloom of evening, pawing the ground, lifting whole antheaps on his tines and scattering the ants and the marl across his back. Leaving one pulverized antheap he leapt a barrier of gorse to visit another area of his domain and landed on a track, in front of a startled forest walker who was walking home. The buck seemed not to see the man, and ran at him and 'through me, if I'd stood still', the man later recounted in the 'Hare and Hounds' at Storton. The Black Buck trotted up the track, squelching water out of the waterlogged clay, his coat blacker than the yews at night.

In November the leaves were hung heavy with frost. By morning they were falling like broken spear heads, heavy and blood-red, or yellow, or as the rust of iron. Their sounds plopping into the ground hid the passage of Capreol, who was moving, a circling of his ground in the Dean Woods, following the excitement of blood and a scent on the air again. He ran half a mile round the woods in the first early morning of the frost-dawn, before robins woke. Caprol had smelt One-Switch's doe. He found a small birch tree calloused down one side which he had raked with his antlers in the summer. He caught the tree and grated all the bark off with the pearls on his antlers which were sharp as small teeth. The tree dropped its two score of leaves that were downy with rime. Capreol ran on to another tree, as the red sun blinked across his body through the beech boles. A hundred yards down through the forest went his shadow running from tree to tree.

Capreol went up through the Dean Woods, scattering the bluebell seeds out of their papery cases. Coming to a ride that led away from his territory he waited, searching for a little scent to give him a way. But the scent of the doe had gone again, for earlier it had tumbled over as in a wave into the fir bottom, where he had first smelt her. But he knew that the wind had brought something and he worked up the wood, through the hazel brakes, with antlers burnished by half a year of fraying, scratched by barbed wire and flints, and made red in that sun of morning.

A quarter of a mile away, in the thickets of young trees and brambles, One-Switch, who had lain up in the early autumn while his young doe had explored the plantation, searched for her again, excited by her scent.

One-Switch had spent a month out of sight of any person, running a small maze of tracks through the plantation but never moving far. Each morning he had left the open rides a few minutes before the grey man's van had passed. He had known where men were working every day, and had lain still once as they came cutting the bushes from around the firs and had crept away on his belly when they were nearly up to him. One-Switch had seen a man climb into the stunted beech one evening, where he had become part of the black twig-faggot growth, not moving, and One-Switch had lain again, more still than death, with eyes held down, although men thought that deer would not look up above the level of the trees, and waited for darkness to let him stand up, when the grey man had gone home.

That day of November spider threads were rising from the fields before midday and catching in the beech trees of the hill-top plantations. The gleams were shot from branch tip and antler point, and Capreol was warm in the sun. He had found the scent of the doe several times, and by afternoon was circling the place where One-Switch was. This was in the wood called New Farm, a mile from Windens. He made a couch by a holly bush which had been cut seven times during the course of a hundred years, yet sent up soft crinkled leaves again from its grey stump. The leaves under the bush were skeletons, which made his bed. He awaited the night. When it was gloom and the hares ran in young frost, he rose and went on quietly through stems of cuttings, finding the maze of One-Switch.

A moon was rising and making leafshine. He stopped to smell the tracks and twigs where One-Switch had thrashed. He knew the scent and remembered the fight under the trees. He stood there for a long while, watching the night and listening with wide-held ears. A noise of rustling grass made him half turn. The sound came slowly through the bushes. A larch leaf feathered white by the moon shook once, and there was another sound of leaves crinkled underfoot, as the animal came nearer. Capreol walked stiffly forward with neck arched, but there was silence under the larch. He waited, but smelling again the scent of One-Switch he ran at the tree, frightening a hare which was nibbling its bark.

For the first part of that night he listened and searched for the buck and his doe. Later he became frightened, being tired, and went back to sleep under the holly bush which made a friendly shadow that slid in broken bars across his back. When he woke it was dark but the outlines of trees were dimly white. The dog star trembled with the first night of winter. Before the robins sang Capreol rose and went back to the maze and found black slots in the frost and the smell of One-Switch on the bracken. He went on down this track where One-Switch had been, finding a place where the older deer had frayed once more. Sometimes he followed by scent in the slots, for the scent was freezing on the bushes.

One-Switch had got up from his couch in the shelter of a hazel stump before the moon had gone, for he had been anxious to follow the doe wherever she went, and she had already left the place where she had couched that night. She had gone four hundred yards and was eating small bramble leaves, and he had found her within a minute. She had taken little notice of him, being hungry, when he came up and touched her on the rump. But he had touched her flank and the spine above her ribs and she had run away from him with a tuft of leaves in her mouth. She stopped to swallow it hurriedly while he followed slowly, sniffing at where she had run.

All this Capreol had seen, for he had run after One-Switch through the tracks in a sort of wild terror, stopping in a stride where the other buck had slowed to sniff at the grass. Then he hid, losing all his burst of courage, and One-Switch trotted away.

The boar badger was there, having been north to

search for a little grain scattered for pheasants in a fir copse, and he was late and was hurrying to get home before the sun rose. One-Switch shook his tine at him and lunged at his flank but the old boar ignored him. The buck pulled some bites of bramble shoots and before they were swallowed ran ahead of the old badger again and lowered his head at him. The badger stopped on his haunches and growled at One-Switch and ran to him and clicked his teeth on the switch tine but he was not really in the mood for this and backed off, unafraid, but wanting to get to the warmth of his deep den and the grass couch. He made a new tunnel track through the bushes which the deer would be unable to follow, and got home forgetting about the encounter.

For two days Capreol followed One-Switch and the doe. But he did not show himself. Many times he wanted to rush into the arena of the ring but the memory of the buck's weight on the bow of his neck came to him again, and he hid instead behind the bushes or ran in the plantation marking his own ground that was without any purpose. The days streamed with gossamer, and in the nights the threads were crusted with frost. It was the moon of the woodcock and fieldfare arriving before the winter of the northern forests. In the morning three fieldfares clacked from a yew tree under which Capreol had slept. They had found the arils, the fleshy fir cone of the yew. Capreol remembered their alarm rattle from the previous winter and looked up when they chattered from the tree top. There was a movement near him, and then a shadow blinking the low sun. It was the doe. But with winter coming, suddenly, the feelings had gone, like the last of the autumn sun.

After this he went by himself into the woods where the rain dripped and ran down beech boles and made the dry places even under the yew trees damp. But there was food still. One evening clouds came down into the trees, and the wind broke a branch off one of the great beeches. Capreol ran from his shelter and out into the rain which darkened his coat. The branch lay still and he went back to it and smelt its green moss and rotted joint where water had seeped to the heart of the tree. The rain broke out of the tree tops and he crept back again into the shelter and licked his fur, and looked at the branch end, which was faintly yellow in the rain-dusk, until it disappeared in the darkness. Through the night the trees pulled at their roots. Up there, above, it was like the boiling of the sea. Water gutted into the peeled bark and fell before his face; he could hear the *tip-tip-tap* on the ground. Under the leaning trunk he was safe. When the rain fell from leaf pools in wind gusts and broke like pistol shots about him he was alarmed, but he did not go. Sometime in the blank night there was a soft sound among the leaves and a hare crept into the shelter with him and shivered behind his back. Everywhere through the forest, all were waiting for the morning.

So Capreol came into his second winter. But he had learnt from the cripple how to keep warm, in that cold spring after his mother was shot.

After a week of rain the moon was seen again, and it was quarter grown and made the sodden ground gleam like dull steel until it went out under the hills. Capreol mooched through the woods of Windens sinking to his dew claws in the ground. One night he crossed the tracks of One-Switch who had passed a few minutes before. He followed them and joined with the doe's slots, foiled in grass along the wood edge. He came upon them in starlight. The doe looked up, and One-Switch stared at him and came across and browsed hurriedly with a sudden nervousness. For One-Switch had lost his tine, and looked like a sheep with his bald head in outline under the stars. They were sheltering under the draughty skirts of the wood. Capreol stayed with them, for all desires had gone from One-Switch, who was exhausted and wanted only to rest.

In a week the skin had hardened under Capreol's antlers and they fell off, and were covered with drifting needles from the larch trees, for Capreol had led the others to Windens, the warm hollow, where the example of the cripple had shown him how to survive the winter. They lived together, interested now only in looking for food and keeping warm.

And in the winter, sometime in the days when the year turned, the watcher walked there and found one of the antlers, and searching around again, found its pair, recognizing the buck which he had followed and watched all the year.

Chapter Fourteen

Rain came again and cloud levelled the hills. The downland plantation became as wild as moorland. The three roe went up the western hill slope of Barrowdown to the yew grove where the ground was drier, and they slept by night for the days were vacant and grey and there was nothing to fear except the coming of winter. There they moved around the edges of the wood, like mist wraiths. Capreol left them after a few days to sleep under the hazel stumps where he had once been with the cripple, a little way down the valley. He remembered the old place where he had been with the quiet buck who had made him feel calm again. The rain soaked into his hide but he dug down into the mould behind the hazel clumps and pressed his back against the smooth bark and slept, while steam rose from his coat.

The moon came and cleared the nights again. The trees were hung with stars, and the leaves tracked Capreol through the nights for they were curled and grown with frost. One night he passed an oak which held Orion in its branches and he stopped and watched. The side of the tree, black against the deep blue of starlight, had moved. The oak was once pollarded with lightning and had grown a bristle of fine twigs like a beard, to hide its bark from the wind when the wood was felled. There was a smooth bulge on the trunk, lit by the new moon half hidden behind; Capreol had seen this part of the trunk move. It was too quiet for a deer movement. The upper stars of Orion's belt eclipsed behind a twig and grew again as he waited. The cripple had taught him to stand and watch, without moving. There was no wind, for the air was frozen still. An owl flew close above the trees, blanking a track of stars as it went. Capreol watched.

Then the side of the oak seemed to grow out and break off from the trunk, and it looked like the outline of a man. Capreol tumbled back a few paces but stopped to look again, so secure were his night woods for him. The thin upright outline did not move. Now he was not sure. So, knowing his woods, he went round the oak at a good distance to get its wind. He kept the small bushes and coppice trees in between, and he went slowly; he watched the oak but saw no movement, nor did he scent anything. He was sliding his way through the woods, hiding, gliding through the open places. He came to a holly bush and the leaves rasped his hair. He stopped and a bird whirred in the holly bush, unable to find a way out in the darkness. He felt the looming branches by their sound for he was not watching his way. The stars of the plough were now above the oak. He moved on. He felt the scabby bark of a hazel stem, briefly, hardly touching it. The moon passed on his left flank. He would get its light behind him. A wickerwork of shadows lay over the trees as the moon came behind his back. Now he looked at the oak again. It was blue-grey. There was a pale patch on its side, showing no more than a tremor of movement. The pale patch afixed Capreol with a great curiosity. He could not move but stood staring, unable to recognize any shape, and he was about to move closer when there was a flick of moonlight on a gun barrel, and he barked.

By the tree, sheltered by the warmth of the trunk, the poacher had stood listening to sounds for an hour. He had heard the movements of rabbits going out of the wood to feed. A mouse had run over his boot. Owls had called, from far off or near, and they had gone hunting, wailing to one another. He was listening for the low murmur of an engine, or the mumble of boots over the hard ground, or a pheasant alarmed. Once, wild duck had passed overhead, close to the stars. He felt a warmth of excitement at winter's coming, and the sport. A woodcock went by; he could see the wings which seemed not to be moving. Then he forgot about the grey man, and when a pheasant rang *cuck-uk-cuck-uk-cuck* in the hardening air it was not because the slow wandering of the grey man had frightened it but a distant rumble of thunder, or guns, or an explosion, which he could not hear himself. He thought to light a fag, but kept still, knowing how the air could carry the smell half a mile. Then, when he was ready to move, seeing the moon rising in fragments through the trees, he heard a sound of dead leaves trampled. He got close in to the tree, thinking it to be the grey man. But when it came closer he could hear four feet moving in the leaves. The sound wandered about. He heard a twig being pulled and knew it was a deer. The animal did not seem as though it could see him. It came close but must have been hidden behind a thicket. He thought of the small shot in the cartridge, and decided to risk a neck shot at close range. Very slowly he moved over to one side to get the deer in view. Then he knew he had been seen. The deer had jumped and then stood still. The slowly creeping moon, like a grub in the sky, showed nothing except the greater darkness of trees. After a while he felt sure he could see the deer moving about; it moved to the left, it came closer, it moved back. But there was silence. He tried looking far to one side, to see it from the corner of the eye, a trick of poachers. But it was no use. He thought of the deer watching him, able to stand for hours waiting for the first move, and he thought of its hot blood on his fingers and the pounds of meat, perhaps a week's wages or a month's meat for his family. He thought to try a shot at a dark place in front. At that moment the deer moved. It was not the relaxed feeding walk. It was the slow walk of the watcher. He heard it in the leaves moving away, then to his left. Very gently he twisted on his heels and followed its movements. It was circling him. He knew it was after his scent, but he wasn't sure where that would lie. As he turned the trees seemed to revolve against the stars. After a while he was facing the moon, and in that second the deer stopped, with its head breaking the outline of the moon. The deer was quite close. The hairs surrounding its two ears were feathered with a light halo. He could see little else of it. It was such a quiet moment. His heart was banging, but the deer seemed unafraid, almost as if it were a dog standing there next to him. He began to raise the gun. The deer barked. The poacher pulled the trigger before the gun was to his shoulder. He saw a column of orange sparks, but nothing else. He ran forward, stabbing his eyeball on a twig, but hardly noticing this; he felt excitedly amongst the dead leaves for the body. It had only been a few yards off. Then he thought to stop and listen, in case the deer was wounded and was dragging in the leaves. There was silence. Again he searched, on hands and knees, feeling between the bushes and coppice till his hands were black with the mould. He had dropped the gun somewhere behind. There was nothing there to find. He stopped and listened again. An owl wailed far away in the woods.

As he ran into the night Capreol followed the paths which he could use well enough without his eyes and ears. The shot sound had impacted his ears, and an orange star floated in his eyes. He felt a pain on his back, but when he stopped in the plantation on the side of the valley of Windens half a mile on, the pain faded. He was unhurt, for the shot charge had gone over his head in a black ball like a swarm of bees. The pain was the old white wound scar on his back, where he had been shot in September, for he thought he had been hit again.

This night made him frightened even of the deep woods, where he had thought himself to be impregnable in the darkness. There had been no warning of that flash and bang. He had not smelt any man or any creature to put him on his guard, so the place itself should be avoided. But there was still somewhere he knew to be a harbour. And he made for it now, leaving the closed woods of the douglas fir valley and the beech plantation and going back through the bracken brakes and the brambles to the cloud valley of Barrowdown Wood, where he had been with the cripple, in the little sheltered pine wood lying just below the down but above the valley of Windens. Now he no longer went out in the daylight but lay like a sodden pine log, seen only by the finches and wandering bands of titmice, and by a brown bird with broad wings and a hooked beak, which flapped and glided in slow unsteady flight about the hills and valleys, for winter had brought the hen harrier south from the pine forests of Sweden.

He found again the tracks or galleries he had known

in the spring. Fallow deer had been there in the summer and torn open the brambles.

A gentle west wind slowly filled the valley at the passing of the moon and its frosts, until warmer air covered the tops of the hills and lay in a pale flood of half-seen sun, without rain, without squall or snow. So December went to the end of the year, and the turning of the earth.

The old boar badger went far on these mild nights; Capreol often saw him. The grey man had put feed hoppers in the valley, which dropped grains of tail wheat into a pile of straw for the pheasants to scratch in. The badger had found these and had turned over the hoppers, knocking the lids off and eating fifteen pounds of wheat in a night, with his family of cubs which were becoming full grown. The cubs grumbled and whined in sleep with wind pains for a day, in the warm warren of chalky gloom galleries many yards below the ground. The badger did not hear them, for he slept in his ball of bitten grass and mosses with his sow, and snored for a day and a night.

From the oaks a mile away mistle thrushes sang and robins called in the darkness. A grey bird sang from a thorn bush in the wild valley, with a half song of broken notes. Sometimes it was hidden within the cloud-mists as it sat still, watching every beetle and small bird nearby. It was a shrike and its bill was hooked into a spine like a blackthorn. The shrike sang, for the sodden air was like the grey rocks and fogs of Lapland. Near Capreol a hedgesparrow crept like a mouse and examined an old bundle of moss growing between two stems, which had been its summer nest. There were fragments of blue shell in the nest, for the hedgesparrow had lost its mate to a passing hawk and its eggs had lain cold until the frosts had broken them. It sang a quiet song, picked up a piece of moss and flew to a pine tree above Capreol, who was asleep. It heard a whistle of air and saw the eye and an open beak, and then twenty feathers splayed in braking like grey fingers, and it sank and fell to the ground and ran about among the twig tangle like a mouse. The shrike hopped down, and Capreol opened his eyes and watched while it chased the hedgesparrow and heard the pattering among the dead leaves around him and the thin shriek of the sparrow's life-end. The shrike was not hungry so it stuck the body on a thorn spine where it sat, and it sang a little to itself as the clouds wetted its feathers like ice fogs.

The year turned. The days were short, the nights long and cold. A greyness was over the land. But the days were creeping towards the spring.

Sometimes Capreol saw One-Switch and the doe. The switch's lance was growing, a stub of fur as grey as lichens on a yew sprag. His doe fed away from him. Capreol knew his own antlers were coming too, and his head was tender.

One night he followed the doe, with his head up, remembering from ancestry some occasion which was to come again in the summer. She slid under the whippy twigs and through deer tunnels with arching brambles which cleavered in his coat. But the twigs knocked his antlers and he crept with lowered head, and forgot the game.

Later in a night of wandering, when the wind had gone to the north-east, One-Switch smelt another deer and went up the hill to the open plain of Barrowdown to see what was there. His doe went after him, following his trail in the dark. It was an old buck whose antlers grew back in cabers like a goat's horns, and were pearled and crabbed with age. Grey-Caber had been shot at by a man sitting in a hide that rested against a smooth larch in the black woods of Marrs. He had run from the woods, frightened by the bullet that hummed away after breaking bits out of a tree nearby. His doe came with him, and they ran half a mile and found some winter barley growing like small green spears. Grey-Caber had an uneven cross of black marks around his neck, which some said were the marks of a wire fence that he had been tangled in years before. He was heavy with age, and his head was always lowered, showing a thick neck. One-Switch did not go near him, but later in the night he walked in the tracks of the doe and followed her upwind with some curiosity. They fed on the barley for the night, blunting the blades, and in the morning they went off that hill and settled down in the west-facing slope, among thick briars and clematis which formed the head of Barrowdown. Somewhere below them was Capreol, resting under the yew tree which was his home now.

One-Switch kept within distance of the two deer in the days afterwards. Grey-Caber acknowledged nothing, but fed and slept long hours of broken sleep, waking often and staring round, always looking for the wind and sleeping again or resting, when the others were restive and ready for moving.

The wind blew snow from beyond the down-top. They came in under the yew trees on the western slope of Barrowdown Bottom and stood with their backs to the wet spate that froze and made them white down to the hocks. Grey-Caber lay down and chewed a cud of dogwood and elderberry shoots which he had bitten off in the afternoon, knowing that the snow would come in the night. The does were hungry; One-Switch found an elderberry bush and scraped at it with his foot and knocked down a branchlet which had small ruby buds. Capreol browsed on short yew twigs growing in tufts out of the crevice of the trunk. In one crack hole a wren hid with six of its babes, now grown like itself into minute wood wanderers with bright eyes and needle beaks, hugging each other's warmth lest the frost nip them. Capreol's black muzzle blew a cloud of warm steam into the hole and the chitty-wren scolded and the babes stared back in terror. A squirrel had scratched at the hole one dawn-break, and they had been too frightened to go out till the sun had arisen. A vixen called on the hillside, and Dogfox answered.

The darkness became wet with a blackness of clouds that took away all shape from the trees. The snow melted and slid off the branches and spattered through lower twigs and broke in cold blobs on their coats. They heard the fox coughing as he tried to bolt a piece of rotten rabbit skin, all that he had eaten that night, for voles had stayed in their earth tunnels in fear of the wet. Dogfox came under the tree but One-Switch struck at him with front cleaves. His smell clung in the air. In the late night the deer lowered their heads and waited for morning.

The sun came now and then in the days of that young year and made Barrowdown Bottom warm for a few hours, and great tits sang from the larch trees above the hills on each side of the valley. Soon it rained again, and the five deer which had formed themselves into a band roved through the bushes feeding on buds, a good rich food in those cold times of late winter.

Capreol found companionship with Grey-Caber, for the bucks' feelings for the does were unaroused. Grey-Caber was alert but always quiet, and Capreol could rest in his company while the older deer looked for danger.

When the moon came full, unseen through formless clouds but making the night opaque, frost came back, but not the glimmer frost of quiet nights when stars tremble. It was a wet frost riming the trees and twigs. It was the worst of winter, which had not yet come that year. A grey east wind reared over the down slope. The deer fed well, but the cold made them hunger. One-Switch smelt grain in the feed hoppers when he was prowling in the valley bottom, and his scraping hoof against the wood brought the others, who were curious. The does stood away in the long grass and bushes, watching while One-Switch struck the side. Grey-Caber waited to see what he was doing but, seeing nothing useful in the knocking and commotion, went away again. Capreol watched, then muzzled the hopper, putting his nose under the lid. Sniffing upwards, he knocked away the lid. Its clatter on the flints and ice-grown chalk pebbles alarmed them but One-Switch returned and guzzled the barley, and Capreol dipped his head in and liked it. When it was empty they turned the trough over, looking for more, and found some in the scratching straw, which had been laid around for the pheasants. One-Switch struck the hopper again, as though it hid more food like a covering of snow.

In a while the night's dull light went, for a black swarm of snow was falling. The deer went back to the yew trees, where Grey-Caber was kneeling in a bed of yew needles. This time the snow laid, and a pinching wind found them. Capreol wandered, finding suddenly that there was no companionship with the two pairs. He wandered a long way, going through to the Dean Woods, making a detour to avoid the place where he had been shot at, recognizing the scents of the six fallow does and their young, which he crossed. Down beyond the pheasant rides the branches of the oaks were laid with snow, like winding frozen rivers. He felt the night cold, so he ran, scattering snow dust off the twigs, and the muscle movement warmed him up.

In the wood, quietly listening to his approach, the hare was feeding, finding mosses and the leaves of wood sedge; the fields were frozen. Over the hare's eyes the fur was white striped, as though grazed by shot pellets. A disease had found him in the autumn and he had hidden in the hedge bottoms, near to death for many weeks, with curved spine ridged with bones. But he had been found by the watcher, who walked quietly every day and dropped food for him, crushed barley with its rich energy, and the hare had got well. It saw

Capreol, it crouched, but knew the animal as a friend when it came closer. It stayed close to the earth, which was warm in the wood. Capreol came up to it, and the hare bucked from its form in a wild exuberance of the night's light, a shining promise of spring light to come. Zig-zagging it ran, galloped down the snow beams, leapt eighteen feet to one side, kicked frost off all the brambles. Capreol lunged his head at the snow and ran away, recognizing the scent of the old hare. In the day the watcher going there from his home in the Dean Woods saw the footprints and followed the snow gallops, recognizing them both.

The frost-bruised earth healed with flowers, first snowdrops and aconites, and all the while the bud bullets of yellow daffodils were rising from underground.

The owl in a hole high up in a beech tree listened to the air humming down through the wooden bole, carrying a wind song to the earth.

YEAR THREE
BROCARD

Chapter Fifteen

Capreol's antlers had grown. The blood had risen and stopped in them. They had dried and hardened. He ran the night and the day's dawn. He broke daylight, for his antlers were his strength and they were nearly perfect. The darkness was afraid of him. Velvet hung in strips, the rags and tatters of winter hiding. He burnished them and worked again, stripping the acrid bark of sallows; the leather of hazel bark fell in shreds. The pearls shone like stars on August nights in his coronets, the two princely crowns which ringed his head. Each antler had three points, all of even length. Men saw them, and marked them, of all the deer in that place. He returned to Barrowdown Bottom, to the wild pine wood and the solitary yews and the warped and stunted beech.

Hiding beneath the thick area of the bushes in Windens' wild places, One-Switch crept about at night. His antler was soft, for it had not finished its growth. Again, it had become a lance, grown long on his head. But it had a backward curve, as though bent with age. One-Switch was in his sixth year. Under the lance the left horn was buckled again like a shepherd's crook and studded thickly with pearls, some of which had joined into larger nuggets of horn.

In the valley, become warm now with early April sun, the five deer stayed, as violets broke in the turf. Grey-Caber basked and slept on a knoll of dead tor grass which had the warmth of straw. His new antlers were bent over like a goat's horns, prickled and encrusted with dense pearls. They had grown closer together, and the velvet of each curled antler touched the other. Grey-Caber's doe was with him always, for her mother had gone when she was half a year grown, chased on to a wire fence by a pair of dobermann pinscher dogs. She felt the comfort of Grey-Caber's old strength. He had courted her, quietly, in the sultry days of August the year gone, and served her in the ring run in the lost meadows of a wood glade, but she carried no young.

Capreol burnished his antlers among the bushes of Barrowdown's old plantation, where the evening sun shone. He had runs which he followed in great excitement, for they were the bounds of his new domain. Then the wet days returned, the hill-tops smoked in mist, and he went back nearer the others, forgetting his wood. Fieldfares, the thrushes from Norway, with mantles grey as hard pine gum swooped into the wood each night. They chackled and called restlessly, watching the light evenings, thinking of the northern lands; but the wind held them back.

At last the wind came warm. Spring grass grew in the

meadows and rides, hiding the backs of hares as they lay out in cloud and sun. It was the real warmth of summer coming soon; even the rain fell warm. The grey shrike flew to the rocky glades and forests of the north, leaving bleaching skeletons of mouse, bird and beetle on the blackthorn spines, which it had meant to eat but had forgotten; the field-fares chattered to one another of the nests of grass, and the grey-brown eggs like smooth lichen-pebbles which they would have; chiff-chaffs came in the oak woods, and willow warblers. Brent geese from the gleaming channel harbours seen from Barrowdown left in the noon of night, for their way was the road of stars which they could follow to their Arctic isles mile by many mile; and their quiet musical *geronking* was heard by the watcher standing in the Dean Woods, who felt a pang for winter gone. The geese went on, over the ancient plain of Anderida, all the time keeping in touch by gentle *geronking* notes until they reached the Norfolk coast, where they rested before making for those Arctic isles.

The six fallow does, sleeping in the Warren, left one dusk, eager for grass on the Manna Ash Down. They leapt the road in twilight and followed paths on to the wood above; crawled under the fence and ripped and tore eagerly at the blue-green sweet grass, juicy with winter's rain. They were black, a half mile away, moving black pools floating and exchanging shapes, easily seen in the nearly dark. By morning they had torn half an acre of grass, showing the yellow roots. The next night they were there again, and the next.

Warmth of the valley made the fescue grasses green in the valley of Barrowdown Bottom, and the roe deer came out to feed in the day, eager for fresh food. One day the grey man carrying a gun came that way and saw them, and stared with hand shading eye against the glare of the sun. The deer did not see him for he was in the image of the sun, and he stayed still for some time before creeping away again. The deer cropped, unawares, for the wind was from the east and gave them no scent from his quarter.

What the grey man had seen filled him with great excitement, and he noted in a pocket book, when out of sight behind the old plantation of Barrowdown Bottom, 'Three bucks, two does. One very good. Three years, perhaps four, antlers ten inches, strong and well branched. Specimen. Other two should be culled. One six years, switch, other seven or eight, gone over.' Later that day he came across the damage done to the grass on Manna Ash Down, which was needed for the cows.

Capreol returned to his wood. In the dusk a shot from far off, near Manna Ash, tunnelled through the air and buried in the valley end. The deer stood alert, and looked about, and forgot.

In the pine plantation, where Capreol spent many hours alone, a small bird called a minute song in the pine boughs above his head, a needle stitching of the air. It hung on a pine cone, and found a tiny spider hiding, and its wings flicking like a moth took it to a twig, where it hid and pretended to fix the straps of moss to hold its cradle nest beneath the leaves. Capreol slid the left point of his head through the bark of a hazel bush, furrowing into white wood. Other parts of the stem he polished with his poll, knocking out a tuft of winter hair. The stem shone reddy brown, like his flank and hindquarters, for the summer coat was coming. He rubbed himself against a tree, helping to cast the last vestiges of the winter coat. Then he scraped the ground, leaving a scent. The golden-crested wren looked with its mouse's eye and flew down to pick in the leaves about his feet. A magpie came to the wood and chattered at the movements below, then forgot them. It sat hunched, drew in neck in a half doze, and raised all its plumage, which moved subdued arcs of sun across the sheen of every blue-black feather, like a bird drawn of gold petals.

The magpie was happy, for it had eaten a nest of blue thrush eggs, and its crest and feathers rose as it relived the anger of the brooding thrush pecking hopelessly at its head with soft berry-eating beak. The magpie opened its beak, and cast a pellet of barley harms and blue fragments. It stared below again, watching the sunlight sliding over Capreol's back and the little bird flitting near his feet, and the magpie considered flying down to see if it were wounded. It dozed, opening eyes to observe pigeons flying overhead or a seagull to which it cocked its head sideways, following the birds' wanderings across the sky with care, for the sea gull had a short neck and head, the hawk symbol imprinted into the minds of birds, making them fear. Once it had been chased by a hawk with wide wings and fierce eye, and had dived into a bush frightening a blackbird which had been grasped by the goshawk's talon. It dozed again, then woke. There was a movement thirty feet to one side in an ash tree. A small bird had landed there with a white feather. It disappeared among the green and grey lichen in a branching of the trunk, and reappeared again. It flew to a branch, and pulled lichen flakes, and took them back to the ash tree. The magpie watched, keeping still. Another bird came, and the two greeted one another with small screedling sounds. The feather bringer watched closely as its mate wove a spider's web into the nest which they were making. For a week they had laboured together, building a mound of lichen like a branch bulge, hollow within, invisible to the wood by its colours and shape. But the magpie had marked the work. The bottle tit flew in wibble-wabble flight, pulling its long tail behind like a cork bobbing on a lake. A quarter mile it went, thinking only of another white feather laying in the gloom of the firs beneath a tree where sat a sparrow hawk on her eggs.

There was a plaque hidden on a tree in the Barrowdown Bottom plantation with the numbers 1924 raised in rusted letters. The plantation had been forgotten, the trees were many years from maturity. They needed no attention for their brick-red trunks had outstripped elder and honeysuckle, bramble and hazel; no men went there. Yet one day there was a scent of a man about the ground and bushes. Capreol sniffed at it on his fraying stocks, and he bounded away and stood some way off, staring at the place, stamping his forefeet. He went back to the others, whom he found by scent. They were feeding on the grass in the rides, and that night he stayed with them. One-Switch kept apart, with his doe. His antler was hung with tassels of fur, the velvet shedding. A piece fell over his eyes, and he scraped at it with irritation. The switch point was sharp, bursting from the velvet like a bud spear.

Grey-Caber was in velvet still. He walked with thick and heavy neck downhung; the black knot-mark of the wire wound was like a shield, carried at the breast. He remained in the cover between the trees. He too had smelt the man. Leading them the next evening, Grey-Caber went up the hill, winding a way among the young trees. Up on a level with the downtops of Barrowdown they could see into the valley, and they couched till the sun levelled the valley with a filling of dusk. The sun was in the tops of the pines on the next hill, when a man's shadow, like a thin giant, raked their place of rest. Grey-Caber saw it first, but lay still, unmoving. The shadow flicked on One-Switch, who stood up. All the others except Grey-Caber then stood too, and stared into the sun. The grey man saw the deer, and did not move. He had not expected to see them there. His shadow crept back to him as he lowered his body to kneel on the turf, placing his rifle down in the violets and thyme. He could see three deer, two bucks and a doe. He noted the switch but stared at Capreol, trying to record each detail of the antlers in his mind. In this minute when a shot could have been fired the sun had fallen among the pine tops of the opposite valley, and the slightest movement of the man was seen at last. Both bucks barked, and turning leapt in opposite directions, the doe scattering also, and the man stood up, not attempting a shot at the switch. He strolled to where they had been, wondering what their food was. He would wait there the following night. Among the little spruce trees he startled another deer, a small doe who ran off without a bark, and then he heard a rustling and switching of the old grass stems, and running forward saw for only a moment the back of another deer crawling low enough to be on its belly. The sound ran through the dead grasses and stopped, and he jumped into the next row of trees and looked up and down. But the thing had vanished. For a long while, till the light had gone altogether, the grey man tried to follow the curious trail among soft grasses, as it went this way and that, never in a straight line although working away from him all the time. He found no clear slot-print to give him the identity. It was a lame deer, he thought, or one that was dragging a snare tied to a branch.

When Grey-Caber had crawled to taller trees that covered over his head he rose and trotted on unseen, and found his doe down in the valley of New Farm Wood. Sometimes shot echoes tunnelled and wandered through the hills from far away below, making them listen for a moment. One evening they crossed the paths of five fallow deer, two fawns and three does, who were making north through the woods away from the fields at Manna Ash Down. The fawns followed the does even though the latter were heavy with young. The fawns had lost their own mothers in the shooting and were blind without the scent of their own kind. They stayed in New Farm, feeling secure. Occasionally the wind brought the scent of man, but they were never sure where it came from, for in those valleys the wind could turn about or tumble in its flowing through gentle gullies that crossed its path.

The grey man made a platform from the old bent beech. The sun was hehind him in the evenings. Sometimes he saw the boar badger come from his hole, grey with chalk-dust. He watched him through the telescope on his rifle, covering him with the black cross etched on the glass.

He moved his sight among the trees, idly watching a small bird with a long tail carrying pieces of moss to a tree. He saw something dark by the tree and moved the 'scope down, and read the iron letters 1924 under the cross. Each night on his return the shadow of North Holte rose over the wood before him and the telescope showed a darkening green of leaves, twigs and bark, lichens, soil and flints. The boar badger hunted for snails in the grass below him in his own secret tracks that only he could see. One night a vixen fox trotted past along a ride and stopped, staring at the twisted beech tree, for the man had lifted the rifle too hastily and knocked the barrel on a twig. The fox had black fur lips; he could see each hair in the telescope. She held her head slightly downcast as if tired out, her eyes stared into his and they were blood orange around the pupils in that red sun. But his own eyes were behind a million years of glass; the fox would never see him. He could see her yellow fangs; her mouth hung open, and the pink tongue moved rhythmically; he thought of it as a useless thing, hunting and wasting food. The fox was panting after trotting hard from her earth a mile below. Tired she was, she had five young hidden in a bury under fir lappings below the hill of North Holte, and her mate lay in a small grave near the grey man's house. The twig sound had cracked her calmness, which was the thought of hunting. Now she could not decide to go on, but waited, wanting to know what was behind the tree between her and her cubs. The grey man placed his cross upon her head and pulled the trigger.

Afterwards he regretted what he had done, for the shot sound splashing over the hillslope and the plantation where he had been waiting for so long frightened the fine-headed deer that he had been watching for, and his view of it was no more than glimpses between the trees as it ran up the hill into the dense cover above.

The grey man did not come back, and Capreol was not greatly alarmed. He knew that he could be invisible, by waiting and watching the long hours of day, standing at gaze, as the old cripple had taught him to do. There was no other deer now on the hillslope. Grey-Caber and his doe stayed in the New Farm Wood, making their territory there. One-Switch and his doe had fled from the grey man to an area that lay in the triangle made by the New Farm Wood, Barrowdown Bottom and the Dean Woods, in an area called Walker's Wood. One-Switch was cleaning away the velvet. He was irritated by the itching and had peeled the sticky bark of ten small spruce trees and walked in the daylight unheeding of anyone, with a crust of gum lodged in his coronets and sticking his hair in knots.

Capreol marked his paths, his own wood maze, a threading back and forth of scent, knotting each at a bush or a sapling, where he scratched and bit, and scraped with his forefeet to secure the lines. He felt a great rage of strength and butted and pushed an elderberry, the weed tree of the woodland, and his neck was corded with muscle, and his cleaves flipped a flint as big as a skull from the ground in the slipping and straining of it all. Other days he lay waiting and sitting mildly, and listening to the living things.

In the dusk overhead the woodcock came, a call-grunt, a whistle like leather squeaking, and the bird flew on, slow wings twining its web among the tree tops, lines laid since the first mild days of February. To the crest of the down it flew, above the plain of pricking lights from houses far below, which went on into the gloom of the city sixty miles away.

At night Capreol tested all the rideways with care, remembering the sound of rifle shots. Sometimes the grey man had come back. He never carried a gun but hurried there with a sack and stopped only to fill the pheasant hopper with barley; once he had looked down into the badger setts and dwelt for several minutes walking round them with care. But his track went by the path, never to one side into the deer's hiding places.

The days drew long, as cuckoos came to the valley and belled the midway air. Capreol knew every leaf and star in his territory. There was an owl there which sat in a tree-nest by day covering a white downy babe with yellow eyes like its own. It had two feathered tufts like ears, for it was the horned owl which called a low haunted note in the winter woods, that few people heard. The hare ran its tracks, and the magpie dropped down through the branches, quiet and shadow-striped by summer, and tapped the hare's young and sucked its pappy brains, as it had done before, afterwards resting and sleeping in its old branch perch near the broken bottle bird's nest, which the magpie had pulled to pieces. The magpie watched, and knew every movement of everything that moved or ever would, as Capreol was learning so to do. So the movement of sun and clouds, snail on leaf or passing hawk, was chronometer of the moving earth, year by year, as few men now recognize.

One midnight, in the scarcely dark nights of June that throb with the call of the fern owl, Capreol smelt another roe deer that had gone through his wood. It was a buck, but not one he knew. He followed in a fast trotting run, stopping often to lick the scent on bushes where he had not scraped. The buck had gone down the hill to North Holte Woods. Capreol ran back along his own track and smelt with care the scrapes and bitten twigs, and keeled bark and all such places where the stranger had been. He ran into his maze and made his markings over again before the fern owl had stopped his song.

The flies had come. It was midsummer. The heat had overflowed the woodland hollows and the young bucks were stirred and running. In a few nights Capreol smelt the buck again. The scent was on a bleak dry wind, rising with the moon. It was from a distance, but Capreol went up the hill where the wood met the barley. He waited by the hedge, not liking the open hill where the moon rolled with one side bloody in the earth. Then he went over and found that the barley nearly hid him. The track went down the field, along the tide edge of barley ears breaking like shining foam at the bank, and he followed the scent through corn spurrey and pimpernel and the odorous pine-apple weed.

Then he came upon a stranger deer, standing looking at the barley sea where the moon was sailing now. Capreol was a silent night creature, he floated, for he had learnt silence. He touched the stranger deer on the rump, and it jumped clear of the corn in fright and stumbled into the field. Capreol watched him, and he turned about, a black silhouette with two small antlers like the feathers of the horned owl between his ears. His name was Bent-Horn, as written in the grey man's book, and this was his first year. He was half-brother to Grey-Caber's doe, for his father ran in the black woods of Marrs, having taken a new doe. He was a little buck, with one antler bent slightly back, and he had run from Marrs Wood in fear. He had wandered outside his home woods and was lost, and between the exciting feelings of his twitching belly he remembered his home woods and the family which had gone.

They had a game of chase and butting, down into the valley woods, but Capreol, coming near his plantation, was too strong for little Bent-Horn and pushed him over. Bent-Horn ran away and laid up in the douglas firs near to Capreol's plantation, sleeping in the cool but open woods unnoticed, like the drift of soft brown earth thrown from a rabbit's stop.

There was another day when Capreol smelt the man. He caught the scent in the same place, near the old beech, on a sultry evening, a hot scent which made him frightened for it was close. He did not stop to bark as a doe would have done, standing to find where the danger was and to warn others. Capreol had learnt of the hot scent of man and he half-crept and dodged low among the chalky plants of sage and vetch, showing little of himself as he crept quietly away to the plantation. Sometimes in the later nights he smelt wandering scents of man until he came to expect them. Others had come to see the fine young buck.

Below in the valley the old boar badger's family of three small cubs were roistering in the grass. Below Capreol, who was eating oak leaves while waiting for the dark, their white masks were luminous. He heard them squabbling – tiny growls and grunting sounds, teeth clicking and sliding on a bone which two were tugging from one another. A third cub, smaller and more nimble, a sow, nipped the tail of one and thus releasing the jaws of her brother from the bone took the end herself and pulled, biting her second brother's nose, running away with the captured bone, hoping to be chased. When her brothers caught her she yarred with tiny teeth and dug, pretending to escape underground. When the old boar badger came out in the dark the cubs went with him to explore the hill and the barley field which hissed when they ran amongst it. Later the sow came out, smelling dew-dull grass, a deer's scent and slugs moving. She shuffled round the cubs' play place, sniffing the leg bone of the old fox, and, finding it distasteful, went north to the barley.

Chapter Sixteen

In July there was great heat. At the farm a mile below Capreol's wood in Barrowdown Bottom the cows clustered under meadow trees in the noon sun. The summer martin felt the cracking mud, and built its gable nest of cowplaps, and caught sweat flies in the milk parlour. Flames of sun-heat shook the distant hills and lifted them until they floated. The woods crackled and burned, and burned until the white flames died in the dusk, and smouldered in the moonlight, black-charred, and were green for only the hour of day beginning.

The magpie sat in the ash, beak gaping in the heat. It had flown five times that day with water for five young held in its beak, from the tank on the down-top; the magpie had swallowed none, and now the water was nearly out of reach, and the five young gaped and cried for more. The magpie was resting, but watching. Below its polished ash tree perch a fly-catcher sat, which the magpie occasionally noticed as it darted into a cloud of flies swarming round Capreol's head below. With its other eye the magpie was watching the grey man walking up the valley path. Once the magpie had seen the man with a gun firing at a crow's nest, and the stick carried on his shoulder on this day looked similar. It sat still, and when the man was close enough up the valley for it to see eyes, mouth, ginger-grey beard, and other features of the face it slipped from the perch without a sound and fell into the air under the ash, opening wings but twice to glide on to the next tree. The magpie retreated from tree to tree, invisible, keeping its nest at the centre of its watching. The grey man was carrying a tin on the end of the stick. The flies crawled on the brow of his hat, his knee breeches were hot, a sweat drip clung to his nose, which was hooked.

In the valley bowl, where each slope met on its fall from north, east and west and the ground was deep with the ossuary of the years, were the white mounds of chalk thrown up by the badgers. The grey man sat and rested, pushing a bone that he found there with his stick into the soft earth, recognizing it for a leg bone of a fox. He found a sharp-edged flint and levered up the lid of the tin, breaking off little sharp flakes against the iron. Out of the opened vessel a coil of odour rose which touched his throat, and he quickly held it to one side and took a red handkerchief from his breeches' pocket to stifle the gas at his mouth. He laid the tin on the mound and dipped his spoon into it, pushing the white crystals from it down into the cool chamber underground. Then he spooned the powder into the other holes of the sett, as the smell rose back out of the tunnel. With his boot he broke chalk and damp earth and nettle roots down into each hole, and blocked it from the sunlight, two centuries of living. He replaced the lid, slung the tin upon the stick, and went away. Capreol saw the figure going but had no scent; he remained curious of it, but slept again.

Below in the ground the old boar knew the grey vapour was coming; he had been gassed before, in another warren. He heard the foot thuds, saw the sun shut out, and heard the gagging sounds of the cubs, which lay still after a little thrashing of dead limbs in a tunnel above him. He ran along another deep tunnel to escape, where a small entrance rose among brambles. But the smell was there, creeping gently forwards. He turned and went on down to a deeper place than he had been for many years, and only a crescent of space remained. The earth was soft, crumbs of chalk were like grain. He flung it behind him, scooping out more with the broad hairy front paws, and forced it again behind until the tunnel was blocked. He dug forward but soon came to the end of the tunnel dug a hundred years before, stopping at a black flint. Here was a chamber with the mildewed skeleton of a badger, its flesh sunk away, amid a black thing of iron that clanked and rattled, fixed to the two back leg bones. The old boar stood on hind legs, pattered with front paws at claw scratchings in the chamber roof, but felt nothing that would be soft to dig. At the flint edge he broke into a chalk seam, feeling the earth's old weakness with one claw. At this crack in the galleries of the chalk the old boar badger worked, scraping away a white dust that was damp and clean tasting. Thirty feet below the sunlight he scratched upwards, feeling the want of air and light, a return to the ground above. Little crumbs broke off; he made a hold for the five claws of one paw, pulling out pebbles of chalk. In an hour he had left the chamber and was lying in a cocoon of air within the chalk, the loose rubble banked up behind, with no smell of the gas but the air bubble he was taking with him becoming dull with use.

Then the boar found another flint nodule, the shape of a great tooth, blocking the way ahead. He scratched it till the tip was hanging out, and then he seized it in blunt and broken teeth and tried to jerk it from its bed. He snapped a piece, breaking a fossil lugworm open to the air. Then he scratched again till his claws were frayed away, and he gripped it once again, and heaved, and pulled, until he felt it nudge him with its weight. At that he pulled again, teeth clicking shut in slipping, starting a snarl through his bleeding gums where two teeth went, but holding on as the million years of weight gathered there, of particles and bones, and fish pieces, and tiny creatures, waited for him in their drowned ocean, where they once had gone to lie forever.

The boar fought hard for his life. He had dug many hundred yards of tunnels in his time, and he knew nothing but work: he was still breathing, for chalk is porous and benign, having lived once already. He wrenched the chalk tumour out of its place and scratched on, upwards, through an old encampment and some bones and flints heat-cracked on a stone-age man's fire of five thousand years ago. The soil was loose now, his great hairy limbs scraped it downwards, he stood on it and forced on through a pan of little flints laid for a hut floor from centuries before. Pieces of charcoal, sheep bones and a chain and the old boar burst into the dew of cool plants, and knew it was night though his eyes were blinded by chalk dust. He lay down trying to smell something that would be familiar, but there was nothing but the smell of gas. Insects and spiders lay dead of it around him, where it had risen and flowed away again. He rubbed his eyes clear of dust and lay exhausted. After a while he went near the old sett entrance and the place where the cubs had played, and saw milky vapour clinging among the grasses and stones, moving imperceptibly in the dark; and he left for a bolt he had dug many years before, for badgers have many resting places.

The smell of the cyanide moved quietly about in the days that followed, and Capreol stayed in the top of the plantation. High summer had come, and the valley was silent. He dozed, but kept waking and turning his head around, imagining sounds of things approaching, to find that a small bird was calling to its young or a woodpecker was tapping a rotten branch. Sometimes he found the smell of man mingling with that of pine-spiced air, and could not escape it. The watcher from the Dean Woods knew his hiding places.

There was another thing that agitated and excited him. It was One-Switch. One-Switch had come into the plantation, though Capreol had not seen him, and had speared a line of small hazels, playing with them and scratching long clear lines, balancing the tip of his single clear point up and down long grooves, without slipping off the stems. Capreol smelt the scents which hung about in the soil, and went along the bushes in the daylight to clean the scents from his fraying stocks. One-Switch did not come back that night, and in the early morning, when night and day were changing in the sky, Capreol went beyond his wood and followed a path to Walker's Wood, where One-Switch would be.

The trees had grown half his height in the summer, and the paths that he once knew in the autumn were tunnels. The brown needles of the spruce branches shook off in his coat and gave him a thick mane of prickles. There were few openings to the sky; here he was hidden. Brambles arched over the tunnels, the raspberry thickets closed behind him. Grasshopper warblers reeled incessant songs from nests of loosely woven grasses, unseen in the thickening stems and leaves. Here he could feed by day and never be seen. So he went on farther into the thickets as the morning came, very quietly, listening, smelling every branch and leaf which crossed the path. Often he smelt the fraying stocks of One-Switch. Sometimes they were old; three days might have gone since One-Switch had travelled that way for he held a great area. The blue gum oozed on the spruce stems and was bloomed with age where he had first made his marks.

At five o'clock he was tired and needed to rest, and he went off the path a few yards to lie in the darkness of a small shelter of brambles like a tent where the ground was soft with fern mosses. But he could not sleep for fear of One-Switch coming on him. Near him was a hare's bones, curled up in a death sleep where it had died nearly a year before. And he tried to sleep while the hare, broken by the many blows of life, watched the sky with open sockets.

In an hour he was rested, with a half sleep of lying still. He was covered from the daylight by the trees, so he went on along the path into the territory of One-Switch. In the sky above he saw the blunt shape of a buzzard wheeling with a raggle-taggle of cawing rooks behind, like the tail of a kite. The buzzard circled back, held on to the small wind and watched, for it had seen a brown slipping shape below sliding among shadows, hidden for much of its travel. Capreol remembered the hawk figure but dismissed it, for he had smelt One-Switch close by with his doe. He came to an open place where the trees were dwarfed by thin soil.

One-Switch lay there, a few yards off in the open, basking. For awhile, as the buzzard moved in the sky, Capreol stood still. The doe lay under a spruce tree, hidden by shadow, but the dusk outline of her face and her black eyes were upon him. He did not know what to do. Then One-Switch turned to look at him and rose, and ran as silent as a spear thrown, and Capreol fled into the tunnel and was chased back to the plantation. He went to his bed of dry dust soil beneath the yew and slept. But it was a poor sleep, often spoiled by dreams.

In the day, dozing, listening for things, something else troubled Capreol. He smelt burning, only now and then, but enough to keep him from proper sleep. Once he jerked upright on sprung legs, waking from a dream of fire and smoke roaring in his head, and he stood swaying a little from sudden waking. But there was nothing in the shadowed wood. Wood pigeons came and went to a scots pine tree near by, beaks filled with water for their young. Far beyond the wood grey pillars of smoke were slanting in the sky like grey fungal stalks growing, forming oval caps of white cloud. The stubbles were being fired in many miles of fields of southern England. In darkness came the bitter smell of burnt earth, and far above the woods the swifts rose on the last bubbles of charred air. Then Capreol again rose from his bed and went in search of the night. He felt an increasing restlessness and he ran past the lines of pine trunks that creaked with old heat, through brambles, feet skidding on dry flints, a great eagerness in him to go to the towrus. He stopped. The night sounded of movement unseen. He ran up the hill along the open track, knowing the moonlight was around him but uncaring that he might be seen. He reached the top and found the tracks of One-Switch in the grass, as he had known he would.

One-Switch was standing in a glade, black and thick as a trunk of burnt wood. He was standing sideways, but drove himself at once at his intruder. Capreol threw his back legs behind just in time, doubling under his neck into an arch, watching the antler spear held out which would run him to the heart. Keeping his eyes on the spear he slipped an inch to one side and caught the crooked sheep horn, and both the deer were flung sideways with the impact. They stood to, each one side of the glade, heads down, eyes showing moon crescents of white, necks corded with muscles. One-Switch waited, holding his strength, feeling the power of the three-year-old. A small moth strayed between them. Capreol felt the soil and stones beneath each foot, and again drove himself at One-Switch in a fierce anger of strength. One-Switch met him, and the spear drove up through the right antlers, his sheep horn catching the other and holding it. Each felt the other's weight and did not draw back, for fear of losing ground. One-Switch was heavier, with a saddle of fat under his hide. He bore down with all his summer weight on to the little baby buck before him, who was a buck to be broken on his territory. And Capreol there, a great rage of strength in him, was stronger, with little fat but muscles which had drawn in lines that could be seen now as he strained. For he had run always, all his life half afraid, and hunted the night, wanting to know the darkness. He felt the weight of One-Switch on his antlers as though to crush him, and he formed a line of one-force from them to his hind toes, which now were gripping in the mulch and soil. His antlers held the weight; for long hours he had prepared himself on his stocks in the woods, feeling his antlers' length and width, their point of touch. They were his senses, more so even than the keenness of his eye or ear; with them he had run the woods and furrowed through the darkness; though yet half afraid with youth, they were his weapons. So now he held them into the darkness which he had known from the first year, balanced them through the bone to his brain, and held them firm. Now One-Switch, eager to end it quickly, tucked his legs down in great bounds, which would have lifted him over an eight-foot fence had he been free. He had the feeling of youth still within his muscles, for he had rested.

The weight bursting on to Capreol's head drove his

hind legs down beyond the dew claws, reaching clay where he could not grip, and the third thrust tripped him back, and he gave stride. But now his feet sinking once again found flints beneath the clay, and there they stayed, gripping on the nodes. So he could not be moved unless his neck gave in, and this was sprung with three years' strength, the muscles pliant as an ash sapling. He matched the thrust, and waited. The magpie was disturbed by the bucks, and glided across to settle in a pine and chatter at them, wondering whether any gain would come of it. Other birds flew across and looked on, some starting fights in their own excitement. Capreol now began a surge of strength to push One-Switch back, and it was One-Switch now who had to hold to the soil, and he did not move, for his was a great weight. So they strained, and then One-Switch felt the strength going, which he had never known before: he was frightened, and pushed, and pushed, and tried to bound, but he was going. His legs one by one gave ground as he was pushed back; he backed into a stump; he held, and tried to push, but Capreol was walking on to him and forced him back on to the stump until he stumbled. He could hold no more. He tried to break away, but he could not break. The antlers, forced and bent apart at the first impact, had sprung in place again. They were locked together.

For an hour Capreol drove One-Switch back, but he rested often, then became alarmed because One-Switch would not turn and run. Their heads hung heavy with the weight, for One-Switch tired soon, trying to draw his head away and run, but he could not escape. So the battle went back and forth, and their mouths were white with foam, and the arena where they had fought, the purple heads of willowherb which had slid about their backs in friendly shade and colour, now were trampled flat and broken into sappy stems.

Darkness came where they were lying, head to head,

and they did not see it. Sometime within the night, when they had rested but not slept, they smelt the doe near and heard her watching them, and Capreol dragged up the head of One-Switch and again they struggled, smashing the thickets of raspberry and bramble, frightening small birds roosting there. They had worked a knot of their fighting back and forth among the trees, and now had entangled it in a patch of willowherb, where it stopped again.

A stem of flowers, broken before the seeding, lay across the back of Capreol, moving with his breathing. The horned owl saw it on his way and wheeled above, and watched their quiet movements, and flew away. A harvest mouse crouched near them, beneath a mat of crushed stems, and listened, ran forward through a maze, ran back, and grappled in its nose with thick scents that dazed its nightly path. It ran again, but was frightened as its footholds moved about with the heavy breathing, so it stopped short, a foot away from Capreol's side, its black round eye a universe of tiny stars reflected from the sky too small to see in human sight, a little world which was a night its own. For many minutes the little mouse waited there, then ran forward a few inches from the deer's hot flank and smelt its naked babes, cold now in their nest entwined to rosebay stems. It rustled into the soft grass to lick their chill, but night moved on.

Capreol saw the stars sliding down the sky, stopping now and then. But refreshed by the cold of dawn they wrestled again. One-Switch moved about wherever Capreol pushed him. Twice he fell back upon his haunches and rose, then Capreol drew back and pulled him to his knees, where he stayed, and they lay still again.

Capreol saw the sun high above his shoulder, and a bright blue beetle crawling near his eye. Then the sun went black, leaving a hole within the sky; yet it had great heat. In the dusk he was cold again, and rain was inside his hair, touching his skin, running down his antlers. He tried to shake it from his eyes, but his head could not move, and his dulled senses had to endure its nuisance. The moon broke the clouds about; a small bird reeled song within his ear; and there seemed to be sun again, and One-Switch, strangely grey, lying with him, grey with dew. He heard the talk of flies whispering in his ear; he listened.

For all that day, long hours upon one another, the flies tangled their dreary tales in his ear, and he had to listen – black beads of flies at his closed eyes – the tales they tell a thousand times: the fly in the silver web that shimmers like a water pool deep in the dark cool, and the flies at the stinking meat of a deer kid, the kid of One-Switch and the doe, that was hung on a wire fence where a dog had chased it; and the flies that look like bees coming and going at the black hole in the ground where the badger cubs had played in cool summer, where the badger cubs had growled through the spring nights: the flies that come and go at the hole the badgers made for their nest of fern and bracken and moss, the clean nest for their young: that died: the rizzling, growzling flies at the deer faeces when they are damp in the dew. The flies were before him, around him, unsure in their eagerness of one body and the next.

The flies talked as the heath flared and exploded with terrible sunlight, making the air shake and quaver. Capreol moved, and the flies heard his heartbeats when they settled again. And all about him the cracking of the gorse pods in the heat, the creak of the pine cones down in the deep shade, and then the flies that encrust the dead shrew nipped by a weasel in the leaf rustle of the glade beneath the beeches, and the black mist of flies that occasionally rise on the whirling eddies of the heat devils and the white humping maggots gulping at the flesh inside the deer's body; and again the silver web that radiates and shivers like a forest pool – all in the heat of the valley. Capreol dozed now and then, awakening to the fearful flies and the sun that rings each hour so slowly.

Then he smelt a man. Capreol was in a glade, the shadows of an oak crossed over and about him, hiding and holding his body in a cradle and binding him close to a warm dry place where his mother had been with him. He must not move, his eyes must never open to look up. He must trust the shadows of the tree and think of nothing. But the shadows had gone. He struggled up and dragged One-Switch with him, plunged into the branches, tore at the weight but could not move it, so he dragged himself into a small darkened place of leaves and mould, and flattened, breathing with a surprising sound he tried to stop. The man was near. He moved about; stopped. The magpie chattered and flew from his vigil bough. Capreol smelt the thing on every breath, and his heart hurt inside his ribs. Then the man appeared. The man came at him, huge, peered into his hiding and breathed on him, and Capreol tried again to break away but again he could not. He smelt the sweating in his nose, as though his throat was torn. Then he felt his antler held tight, his head pulled about, and a pressure on his skull at the antler root, a grinding as of bone breaking, sawing into his brain. When he woke again the man was standing over him, and he kicked in fear, and rose up, all the weight gone from his head, staggering from the imbalance, and tottered away, hiding, hiding, under hazel leaves, under raspberry thickets, on and on, beneath a spray of honeysuckle, through the low feather stroking green soft needles of the little firs, into tunnels of darkness that could not be followed, into a place that only he knew of, and would never be seen by man till all this had changed.

In the glade, smelling of the crushed plants and

flowers like purple bruises, the watcher stared in wonder at the place and the tangles of fighting which had gone half way down the hill. And he lifted up the head of One-Switch, which was scarred with white marks, and found old weals of wire along the legs, and a broken cleave, and an antler like a lance; and he took hold of him and dragged him to the pine trees where the soil was soft.

On a wire fence, on the skyline of Barrowdown, a corn bunting skirled a song, hardly heard. There was the sound of wood doves half a mile away in the firs, and there was nothing more during those August days. Nightjars had gone and the swifts were over the Aegean, a thousand miles away, and there was silence: a blue still sky, and Pleiades rising in the midnight woods.

Capreol lay still in his great weariness and slept for a day, after first creeping out by night to the half empty water trough on the hill field, drinking deeply to replace the moisture in his shocked body. Slowly consciousness of the world filtered through, and he watched from his pine walls, which he knew; he watched. He went into the spruce trees. Nothing there. His legs were stiff, his neck ached, and it hung low like an old deer. Bracken broke, his pushing flattened it as he cut a new track. For a day and a night he circled among the trees, often resting, avoiding the old ways. He found the fighting place, and smelt it all carefully and went up the hill. There was nothing. He ate bramble flowers and listened to the morning coming, and walked on with half-eaten fragments in his mouth. Near the top he heard movements, and a flowering of anger made him run towards it. It was a deer. She was playing a game and had made a circle of trodden earth in a glade where some birch trees were eaten to runted shrubs, an old place that deer had known before.

The little deer continued, aware that he was there. She was running a circle, and going on, another, forming a figure of eight around two birch trees. She stopped, and he heard her soft breathing and a whirring summer moth beyond. The morning was not there, yet, for any person watching, but he could see, and he knew the deer from her scent, her shape and her running ways, as now she went again among the birches, a looping in and out that mazed him and made him still. But in that green August morning, where men saw only shapes, if men were anywhere about, the two saw clearly, and Capreol moved, and joined the running, and followed her, and the sun rose again.

Days of a wind-blown heat followed, when the cornfields on the down-tops turned white. The woods were grey with the weeks of summer's dust. Nobody was there among the down-tops, and they knew of nothing but the waving grasses grown as yellow flax, and the warm wind, coming by dusk, by starfall, and by the tide-flowing light again. It was their place; and it was the only place. They saw their shadows break, and fall again by dark, and they ran together.

The stars wandered through the grey plains of night. They were seen by no one, but once the old boar badger searching for barley on the down-top bumbled about along their tracks, following the threaded scents of snails in dew, and they remembered him and he remembered them, and he hunted for blackberries all night among their scent, some little way downwind, finding a comfort in their nearness.

So the quiet nights came, and went, until the stars shook in the late sky with a feeling of cold, and wild ducks came over touching the stars.

And the ring became circles of dust, and a yellowhammer sang from the birch tree. The doe went quietly, keeping to herself, waiting for the feeling that would come, one day after leaf-fall, when life would begin in her, that was now only waiting.

And so the buck, too, on his own, quietly lying in the woods, resting, hearing the doe often, sometimes meeting her or finding her scent; knowing she was there.

Chapter Seventeen

Lying there before first light in those last summer days he was grey as the pine boles in Barrowdown Bottom, but at the dawn he became foxy red when the pine crowns were still black. Capreol had a bed of pine needles in a glade which was warm in the morning sun. For two days he basked after the first chill rays had found a gap in the canopy of the old bent beech nearby. Here he drowsed, flicking his ears and flanks continually as flies found the warm dewy coat. A single blackberry had ripened in the glade among the branches of green and red berries which were like sour little warts. The berry hung in the centre of the sun-pool and attracted a foraging bumble-bee which had come in the dawn dusk from a mossy nest near to the old badger run. The bee prodded the juices with excitement, scrambling back and forth with wings a-shimmer, making a frail whine. Soon it had drunk, and flew off, a tiny woodland Bacchus.

In a while a solitary meadow-brown butterfly which had wandered through the pines two days before awoke beneath a bramble leaf, and flexed wings three times before flying sluggardly across the glade in search of nectar. Sunlight reflected from the berry: the butterfly dropped with closed wings to feed. As the sun rose higher hoverflies darted through the glade and whined above the buck. Blow flies droned up from the damp leaves and settled in groups about the pine boles, clinging close on the bark, positioning blue hairy bodies to feel the heat of the sun. When the night chill had left them they chased one another in rapid circles and loops around the sunlit trunks, settling for an instant to bask before buzzing away again in wild tangles of flight. Above them the hoverflies hung at their pitches, darting at the flies if they came into this higher territory. A drone fly with heavy bumble-bee-like body, white-furred and with black spots on its wings, landed heavily upon the blackberry upsetting the meadow-brown. For a moment the brigand fly sucked at the juice, then zurred away. By now a cloud of small black flies had gathered on the buck's ears and eyes. He shook his ears; the black halo rose for a second, then settled, probing into eyes and nostrils with dabbing tongues. Capreol turned to his flank and ran a thin tongue, like a whip, among them, and dried the dew from the foxy coat so that his odour was dulled.

The sun had awakened three large butterflies whose colour matched his own, a colour bright for forest glades but broken up with black lines and patterns. The fritillaries glided among the trapeze-hanging hoverflies, in and out of the sunlight, past the ravelling flies. They weaved a dozen pine trunks into their scent patterns, and even frittered at the cold pouring sunlight that tumbled around the old beech, outside the glade. Sometimes a fritillary would plane down from the procession to alight on a flower.

When the sun left the glade around mid-morning Capreol was left in the deep shade of pine trees, a clearer coolness than he had found in the yews or beneath the beech or oak trees. The shade here was fed by a steady moving of air through the conifers, an air filled with pine gum scent and the crackle and bursting of cones as the sun rose higher. On hot days gum ran from old branch scars of the scots pines and blistered red on the branches of their flattened crowns, giving warmth of colour like old bricks.

When autumn had held the land for many days, and spread its slow fire through the forest; when autumn held the land, one day winter came to take away the fire. There had been gales and a swirling of mist among the beech hangers that autumn, when the woods were black with the rot of rain; but the winds were autumn winds, warm and soft, sometimes with salt from the sea to help mellow the leaf. The umbrous fire had not been quenched in rain: it smouldered like the woodman's charcoal pyres in the glades, with a glow that turned deeper red. Sometimes on fine days after frost when the fallow bucks groaned in the woods of Blackbush and Bey Hill the fire had begun to crackle.

One day there came a grey wind that had not been felt since the seasons had changed at the time of the blackthorn blossom. It was a wind that shocked with its cold, that silenced the midday choir of muted thrush songs and stripped the elder of its feebled leaves. Pheasants crept to the deep wood to search for food; blackbirds were blown into the thickets; the wren crept into the darker crevice.

Within the grey wind was the smell of snow, for the wind had come from the north, and the fire of autumn became an ember heavy with ash.

The wind came in across the bare chalk uplands and flailed the forest for two days. For a week the leaves fell and the trees became thin again; on the seventh day the wind slackened in the afternoon and in this moment a sun of great brilliance set the woods afire again. It burnt in the valleys and up the hillsides through the beechwoods, roaring through every tree until the forest from London to the Channel coast was ablaze, and as evening came the valleys were left charred and cold, and the last fire of autumn burnt out in the beech hangers high on the downs. The sun became a small red ember deep in the forest: when it had gone, winter was there.

Capreol and the doe were in the wild tops of Barrowdown Bottom, always together, following one another's slot-prints, wandering in a red gloom of fog which was day in the twilight end of the year, for the sun had gone. One day the valley appeared below them, and they came out again into hidden day, where the yew trees were smoking with wet fog.

The wind wandered, and in the afternoon fog shadows stole among them and trees moved and faded, and six deer shapes came by them with no sound or smell. That day the year turned.

And with the New Year came frost and snow for many days. One afternoon, late, two men came into the valley woods of Windens. The men were car-breakers from the city, rough diddycoys, living off their wits among mounds of rotting machinery. They were comforted in this wild place by the orange sodium glow from street-lamps fifteen miles away, which gave the snow the faintest colouring. They had parked a van a mile away, and they had come to look for pheasants in the wood, knowing it to be a lonely place where they could hide among the trees along the side of the valley and never be found by any grey man. The men wore dark blue working coats; they forgot the direction of the wind and walked with their backs to its icy strata along the valley, so that pheasants saw the dark figures and flew up or smelt them and ran alarmed into the shelter of the bramble thickets along rabbit runnels, long before the men appeared. The men were excited. They had come right through Windens and were in Barrowdown Bottom. They stopped by a clump of yew and made a plan to encircle the thickets and to drive the birds towards each other. They stamped their feet and did cabby's warms and then they lit fags and one of them spun the match away and watched it land in a hole in the snow, where it sizzled out. The man looked closer, catching his friend's arm, and saw that the match had landed in the enamelled slot of a cloven-hoofed animal. They looked at each other.

'Sheep, is it?'

'Deer, boy-o.' He looked about. 'Bloody hundreds of them.'

Capreol and his doe had fed on the yew and dogwood there nearly all night.

'You know how much they fetch in town! People round here eat deer meat.'

'We'll never get them with these pissing things. We need candle-wax in these pellets to make them stick together, like a bullet!'

The next evening there were four of them. They had made a plan, for they came quietly and carefully up the wind. That morning they had picked open a score of twelve-bore cartridges and poured hot candle-wax onto the top of each, turning the hundred and eighty small lead pellets that would merely sting a deer at twenty yards into a fused shapeless slug that could tear a hole through its body.

This time they had dogs, two wild alsatians that spent their days on the ends of their chains prowling beaten tracks of mud among the ruined cars, gasping half-throttled barks at everything they saw. The men had taken turns at holding the leads of the half-wolves, which had rasped with strangled breath all the way up the white valley. The night before had again been very cold, and new slots showed distinctly as blunt holes through the snow crust. The two men pointed to the enamelled ice-casts, and their companions whistled and blew into purple-cold hands.

'What are we going to do if we shoot a cart-load?' asked one excitedly.

'Get the bloody dogs to drag the buggers out, like they nearly dragged my bloody arm out.'

Redwings flew over as the sun, setting beyond the island out at sea, began to turn the snow to the strange orange colour that would last into the night with the distant street lights.

Two men went forward along a side path; the other two waited with the dogs. They whistled to one another, and let the dogs go.

The two half-wild animals had never been in open country before. They had never been off their chains for more than a few hours in their three years of life. They ran into the maze of rabbit, hare, deer, squirrel and pheasant scents and charged wildly back and forth. One dog accidentally landed on a half-grown rabbit which it tore to pieces. Another chopped the tail of a squirrel caught in the open.

Capreol and the doe were lying up in the clumps. They had heard the wheezing of the dogs and the sibilant voices of the men, and the doe lay head to tail and listened. The buck kept alert, the doe watched. Snow steps came by them. Cold scent of men, bitter scent of tobacco. People had been by before, once or twice in the week, sledging on the hill. Silence. Then new sounds, bushes shaking, tapping. And the fast breath of dogs running. Whistling, and low *hi, hi, hi.*

Capreol stared at the white lattice of twigs and snow, and remembered the sound from before.

Then he heard a crashing of undergrowth, and snarling close by. The deer leapt up, and losing the entrance to their den in panic were blocked by low branches and matted brambles. At that moment a dog came into the entrance and the buck leapt round to face it, kicking out with his sharp cleaves. The dog's teeth snapped at the sinews of the buck's neck, but only for an instant. Again Capreol struck out with his front cleaves. In the two seconds of this encounter the doe had found a patch of clear sky above for which she aimed, and leapt through, a great leap four feet above her head like a bird in flight, which Capreol followed, as a shot went with a hum over their heads. But as they passed the beech tree a man stepped out and fired and Capreol saw the doe fall to her knees and thrash wildly about throwing up reddish snow, and there was a second shot and he felt something hit his side, but he ran, and took the cold air in his nostrils and flew in bounding leaps over the snow, away, away, for ever.

And when he had gone the men tried to follow his marks for a short way but it seemed that he had only touched the ground here and there.

The men clubbed the doe as she thrashed and struggled in the snow. They cut down into her belly and pulled out the guts, and buried them in the snow.

Afterwards, in the night, late, in that glade where the orchids would one day be coming, a fox which was passing in the night drew downwind a mile to a smell it knew well, which sidled up the hill; and finding the glade it dug from beneath a pile of snow a skin ball of bramble buds, which it ignored, and digging a little deeper, it picked out a tiny deer, strangely white in the darkness, with swollen eyes, and cleaves, and dew claws yet specks of gristle, and a muzzle no bigger than a mouse's lips, a tail like a slipped skin lizard's, and two buttons upon its head, where antlers would have been.

Capreol followed a frozen wind that broke among the ash boles of the Dean Woods. He was unaware of the way he had taken. There were stars sliding through the branches above, and the twig buds were cloven, like the tiny feet of deer. And he followed the frozen wind from the old coppice woods of East Holte and crossed the down at Manna Ash, and followed the streams of air that sluiced between tree boles or the running darkness of the hedgerow. After the high down he came into a wood at Stonerock. He smelt a dog scent, and somewhere he heard a chain rattle and a dog starting to bark, and he ignored it.

Often then he lay down in the silence of the night, but rose again and, not eating, set out for the path which passes along the lower fence line of the hill. The brambles were grown over in arcs. Many times he stopped, unable to break through. But going down slowly on his knees he pulled himself under on his belly. Stretched out thus, he once could not rise again, but lay still and, with eyes closed, dozed, and images went through his mind of a quiet, dark place. Small snow crystals fell here and there and made the land grey. Later in the night he went on, the bramble thorns catching on his hair and his cleaves rattling on the old ash keys.

He came to a crossing fence and stopped before the wires. He lowered his head, but could not move before this barrier. For a while he rested; the scents and sounds of night had lost any meaning, and the sallow willow bush with its acrid tasting bark went unnoticed. Then he went up the fence, but there was no gap and he followed for a mile until he came to a small crab apple tree growing outside the fence, smooth with cattle rubbings. The tree had sheltered a bramble and a spindle tree, and a partridge nest in summer. He tried to eat a few leaves of the brambles, but lay down heavily in the dry leaves. The Black Buck of Bey Hill and his does passed that way; they saw him and quickly moved away, knowing what it was they saw. In the night a great wind arose and more snow fell, and before the morning came he moved and broke open a casting of ice grown on his back. The heavy movements woke a hedgesparrow which crept down into the thickets fearing the grip of wind. The death-watch beetles lay silent in the old ash post. Capreol knew that he must go on, away from the tree and the open hillside. He slanted across the field, and his tracks wandered in the snow but were blown away. The wind covered and uncovered black straw, blackened by an autumn fire of stubble, and hurled it on, away past him, and the stones became smooth and grown with a layer of ice along one side, as were his legs and coat. And there was, somewhere in the field where he passed, a red stone, broken by the fire. Its many million years of life were gone, and so would the world be gone, soon.

He went on, finding a tunnel that he knew, going down among the yew branches. He passed a black bower of shelter, where there was a piece of iron grown to many times its own thickness with the ice, and a bottle in which a mouse had died. He rested for a while, as the ghost glimmer of headlights from far below lit the shelter, and he felt the hill wind searing the bushes, and went on down, and came into the valley of Kinzerlic.

A falling night; a falling sky – Capreol lay in darkness, under the yews, wanting to rest. Snowflakes broke among the twigs and fell in pieces, moving down with feeble wander to touch his coat without feeling. It snowed through the night to the dawn, until the great yews in the valley of Kinzerlic were mantled over.

And in the morning Capreol was in a green cavern,

as though within the sea; and he lifted his head and the sun broke, somewhere beyond, a long way off, and there were splintered colours above him, and silence, and he was held; and he knew that he must never move.

And in the spring, when the ice had broken from the yew crowns of the valley of Kinzerlic, the watcher passing quietly in those woods knelt and stared at the circle of bones; at the little skull tucked down to the last white fragments of the backbone; and he wondered, moving the bones with his stick, not recognizing them and finding no reason for it all.